The Killing Time

Logan Winters

A Black Horse Western

ROBERT HALE · LONDON

ISBN 978-0-7090-9183-7

Robert Hale Limited
Clerkenwell House
Clerkenwell Green
London EC1R 0HT

www.halebooks.com

Typeset by
Derek Doyle & Associates, Shaw Heath
Printed and bound in Great Britain by
CPI Antony Rowe, Chippenham and Eastbourne

ONE

You could tell he was a man by the two legs and two arms, his mouth and nose. Even his protruding red eyes were somewhat human, and someone had dressed him up in man-clothes, no matter how filthy his jeans and torn blue-checked shirt were, so the overall image of John Bass should have led you to believe he was a human being. He was, of course – but his standing there with his mouth half-open showing broken yellow teeth, hunched forward with his thick hands hovering over his holstered Colt revolvers, caused Tom Dyce to wonder what sort of animal he had come up against. Bass didn't breathe so much as snort in and out through his wide nose; he didn't so much speak to a man as grunt at him, and the grunts were not pleasant. He seemed to have difficulty saying more than four letters at a time. Bass was big, sweaty and had a sickly smell about him like a dying bison. His face was covered with black pores as if he had taken a blast from a shotgun loaded with pepper full in the face. The hair on his forearms was more like fur than human hair. Outside of that, Dyce supposed, he was probably a friendly, upstanding citizen.

Tom Dyce was ready to give any man the benefit of the doubt, and would have if Bass hadn't grunted out his strong desire to shoot Tom Dyce dead.

Tom Dyce had come to arrest John Bass, but Bass seemed unwilling to go with him, even though he obviously belonged in jail, if not in a pen where people could come to wonder at him and children could be taught lessons in abiding by the law and the importance of hygiene.

'It's just that you're not welcome in the town of Rincon,' Tom Dyce said. 'The marshal wants me to lock you up while he decides what to do with you, and I have to do what he tells me.'

'Why?' came the growl.

'It's how I make my living,' Tom Dyce said and Bass's body began shaking with rumbling laughter.

When he had quieted, he growled again:

'No. Dyce, it's how you get dead!'

People in the saloon began to back off in various directions. They had gathered for the amusement, but lead flying around in the small room was not entertaining. No man in the saloon doubted that Bass would draw. He had proved his willingness to shoot on multiple occasions, most recently the day before when he had gunned down two unarmed Chinese, apparently only because they were available targets.

That was the incident that had prompted Marshal Joe Adderly to send Tom to the Silver Strike saloon to face Bass. 'Frankly,' Adderly had told Dyce in confidence, 'I don't care if you shoot John Bass in the back through an open window. Just get him.'

Tom Dyce considered Adderly's advice as Bass stood hunched forward, glaring at him with those red eyes. He half-wished he had ambushed the man as the marshal had all but suggested, but even shaggy wild animals deserve a chance.

'Put your guns down,' Dyce said and the men around him smiled. Even Dyce knew that was no more than a weak joke. Bass wasn't going to surrender and walk over to the jail. It wasn't in him to go easily. Dyce was thinking: 'If it has to come to this, I've at least got a better chance in a gunfight than going knuckle and skull with John Bass,' who could probably tear him apart like a baked chicken.

'Listen, Bass. . . .' Tom Dyce tried again, but it was too late for last chances. Even as he opened his mouth to speak he saw one of Bass's bear-paw hands drop toward his holstered gun. The big man fired and Tom Dyce felt a tug at his belt as a bullet passed his body, missing by only that much.

'Oh, the hell with it,' Tom muttered. He slipped his own Colt from its holster and fired back. Gunsmoke filled the room now, floating up in black wreaths toward the low ceiling. Bass did not fire a second time. He couldn't. John Bass was sprawled against the rough floor of the saloon. A few men stepped forward to congratulate Tom on his shooting as he stood over the fallen form of John Bass. When he had entered the saloon, the customers had jeered Dyce. After all, no one wanted to offend the killer, and Bass had been buying the drinks. But the winner is always cheered, and Tom Dyce seemed to have bested John Bass.

Tom nudged Bass with his toe and it was as if he

had prodded a dead man back to life. A hunter himself Tom Dyce should have known better than to assume the grizzly was dead and not just stunned.

Bass came up on hands and knees and thrust his skull up into Tom's crotch, doubling Dyce up. Tom Dyce backed away, seeing that his pistol had flown free, as had that of John Bass. And now Bass was on his feet, panting and snorting, stalking Tom across the saloon, his ham-sized fists clenched. Tom glanced around for help, but it was obvious that no one else was willing to risk John Bass's wrath. Tom backed away, his hands held weakly up, until his back met the wall. He could see the blood on John Bass's chest, see beyond his shoulders the unperturbed bartender in his white apron, calmly rinsing his glasses while there was a break in serving drinks.

Bass roared and lunged at Tom Dyce.

Bass threw a big circling right hand against Tom's ribs and Tom felt something crack. He had his own fists clenched firmly now that the wave of nausea from being hit in the groin had passed. He tried jabbing, pawing at Bass, feeling like a child. He couldn't get the space to find the leverage he needed, pinned against the wall as he was. Bass in the meanwhile continued to drive punishing blows with the weight of his massive shoulders behind them. He wasn't fighting like he was the gun-shot man.

Tom put his fists in front of his face, ducked and wove trying to avoid the big man's fists, but if Bass was badly wounded, he didn't show it. He was relentless, pounding Tom's body with fists that landed like anvils. Desperately Tom tried kicking his attacker's shins, stomping on his feet, clawing at his eyes. None of it did much perceptible damage and Bass continued to buffet Tom's body, occasionally landing a head shot. Tom could feel blood leaking from his ear and dribbling from his nostrils now, and he knew he had no chance if he remained pinned where he was. Their faces were close together. Tom could smell the strong buffalo-scent of the big man, see those bulging eyes which seemed to have no intelligence behind them, see the gaps in Bass's broken yellow teeth. Bass took half a step back to load up for a finishing shot from his right hand and Tom seized the moment, kicking Bass on the kneecap with all of his remaining strength. When Bass grunted and staggered away just a little, Tom ducked under Bass's arm and slid aside.

The Killing Time

Tom Dyce, a peace-loving man at heart, is deputy marshal of Rincon and the right-hand man to Town Marshal Joe Adderly. Knowing a thing or two about wielding a gun, Tom is the man Joe trusts when real trouble arises.

However, Aurora Tyne, the woman Tom loves is in real trouble: her new foreman has taken to rustling her beeves. To make matters worse it is rumoured that he is in fact the notorious bank robber, Vance Wynn.

Now Tom heads for the Thibido country to come to Aurora's aid, not wishing to use his guns, but knowing that there always comes a killing time. . . .

Bass howled like the wounded animal that he was, and charged in Tom's new direction. Tom Dyce saw his opportunity. He felt behind him and gripped a chair, and as Bass trudged forward, Tom swept the chair up and then brought it down with all of his remaining strength.

It was a good chair of solid oak. It did not crack or split, but John Bass did. His fending arm was broken above the wrist and his cheek split in a long, jagged gash above the cheekbone. John Bass went down again.

'Should have shot him again when you had the chance,' a man said, handing Tom back his Colt. Everyone was suddenly his friend again. Tom took the pistol, turned his head and spat blood.

'Give me some rope, bartender, or a few bar towels – whatever you've got.' He would not let Bass become conscious again with his hands untied. After trussing the big man's hands, sparing no energy as he tied the knots, Tom took an extra bar towel and wiped his face. His nose continued to bleed, his ribs to ache. He looked around him and saw no one he could trust to help him escort Bass to the jail, so he holstered his revolver and crouched down to try to pick Bass up from the floor. Lifting 250 pounds of dead weight proved to be beyond him just then. As he rose, panting, two men stepped forward, willing to help him that much. They threw Bass over Tom's shoulder, and he staggered toward the batwing doors of the saloon, the unconscious bear weighing him down. As he left, the drinking men were already at the bar, ordering fresh drinks, the moment's excitement ended.

'That's it, Joe,' Tom Dyce told Marshal Adderly as he sat in a wooden chair in the lawman's office. In the cell he could see John Bass, fitfully sleeping, his hands now secured with manacles. 'I'm quitting the game.'

'Because of one rough night?' Adderly asked. He was a narrow man with thin reddish hair, not meek, but very careful about the way he approached trouble. That usually involved sending a deputy to do his work.

'Because I can't see any profit in it,' Tom groaned, bending over. They had sent for a doctor to see to his ribs and to Bass's wounds, but they knew that the doctor was a drinking man and might be hard to rouse at this time of night.

'You know, Tom,' Adderly said in a fatherly tone as he leaned back in his chair, his cupped hands folded together on his lap, 'I took you in and gave you a chance when you were down and out. You were grateful enough to have the job then.'

'Yes, I know, Joe. When you're flat broke, fifty dollars a month sounds like fair pay.' He shook his head and wiped back his dark hair with his fingers. 'After you have a little silver in your pockets, you start to wonder.' To wonder if he had become nothing more than a hired gun for a cowardly marshal, Tom thought, but did not say aloud.

Adderly rose and walked to the cell to glare at the massive form of John Bass. 'Why didn't you just finish him off when you had the chance, Tom? It would have saved you a lot of grief.'

'I don't know. It just didn't seem sporting,' Tom said as Joe Adderly returned to perch on a corner of his desk. 'I never killed anyone in cold blood.'

'I understand, but do you think a man like John Bass is ever going to say to himself, "Gee, Tom Dyce could have killed me but he didn't. I ought to thank him." '

Tom found enough strength to grin. 'I don't suppose so.'

'A man with a badge has to do what he thinks is right, but, Tom, he also has to survive. There's no wisdom in being a suicidal lawman.' Adderly stretched his long arms. 'I suppose I should have gone after Bass myself, but I knew you could handle it. Besides, as you know, I have a wife and two sons to think about. What would they do without me?'

'I don't hold your sending me over there against you, Joe. Where's that damned doctor!' Tom called out as his cracked ribs sent a surge of pain through him.

'He's probably on the way. What you're saying about quitting me, Tom . . . are you sure this isn't something that might pass in the morning when you're feeling better?'

'I've been thinking about it for a while, Joe.' Tom shook his head heavily. 'No, I've decided – I have to get out of the business and ride somewhere where I can find work that doesn't involve blood and killing.'

Joe Adderly nodded meditatively. 'I think I know what you mean, Tom. This is a hell of a way to earn a living. Puke and blood and fighting. I think if I were a younger man I might consider quitting myself and just riding off.' His eyes grew distant, then he yawned. 'But you know, I've got a good deal here, and there is always my wife and two sons to be considered. . . .'

'I know, Joe,' Tom said a little snappishly. His ribs were hurting, his head had begun to throb dully. He closed his eyes briefly and thought about going home and sleeping without waiting any longer for the doctor, but he kept his seat. The hotel seemed a long way off. He wasn't sure he could even make it that far.

'Tom, have you any idea how you're going to make out after you leave Rincon?' Marshal Adderly asked, rising to walk to his creaky filing cabinet.

'No, Joe. No, I don't.'

'Well, a man has to have something in mind,' Adderly said, slipping a sheet of paper from the cabinet. He returned. 'This might be something you could get your teeth into.' He handed the paper to Tom Dyce.

Tom scanned the Wanted poster – for that was what the paper was – briefly, then shrugged and asked Joe Adderly, 'What's this to me?'

'I thought it was something you might be interested in. Look. Tom, where are you planning on riding after you leave Rincon?'

'Back to the Thibido region, I suppose.'

'That's what I figured. Thibido is near to Flagstaff isn't it?'

Tom Dyce rubbed his tired eyes and answered,

'Not what you'd call near, but Flagstaff is the largest town anywhere close, yes.'

Marshal Adderly returned to his desk and sat down as if he were finished talking, but a lot was left in the air between them. 'You never had much luck making a living up on the Thibido, did you, Tom? Else why would you have come down here?'

'I didn't have much luck,' Tom agreed, leaning back to hold his arms tightly across his ribs. Adderly had started those old thoughts again. Thoughts of Aurora Tyne, whom he had only just begun to forget. When he had left Tom had harbored hopes of returning to her one day with his pockets full of money. Such is the way of life – he was sitting broken and battered in a shanty town with almost enough money to buy trail provisions on his ride north. 'What are you thinking of?' Tom Dyce asked, not sure he wanted to know.

'Vance Wynn – the man on that poster – is reported to be up in the Flagstaff area. If you didn't read the whole poster, he robbed a bank down in Ruidoso some months back. Made off with a good bit of loot. You know that even if I wanted to, I couldn't look for him, my responsibility being toward this town.'

'I know,' Tom answered dully, grateful that

16

Adderly had, for once, not brought up the fact that he had a wife and two sons to worry about.

'Sheriff Harley Griffin out of Ruidoso has been trailing Vance Wynn for a long while. He's in town right now. But he also has other obligations. It seems there's a range war looming down there. He's going back to Ruidoso, giving up on Wynn, who's far out of his jurisdiction anyway.'

'And so you are suggesting that I go after the man?' Tom asked in disbelief.

'I'm not suggesting anything,' Adderly replied with a weak smile. 'It's just that there might be a chance in it for you.'

'I'm not a bounty hunter; I'm not going to continue being a lawman.'

'No, Tom,' Adderly said, holding up a hand. 'I know that. And just now you're tired of being beat up and shot at. But say you did happen to run across this Vance Wynn? There's a good description of him on the poster.' Tom found himself involuntarily scanning the Wanted notice smoothed on his lap.

'Tom,' Adderly said, comfortable in his chair again. 'Don't you see what else the Wanted poster says. They're offering two thousand five hundred dollars for Vance Wynn. It's the biggest reward I've

17

ever seen put up. They want him bad in Ruidoso.'

Tom nodded, his thoughts drifting briefly away again to Thibido, to Aurora Tyne's smiling face, her dark hair drifting in the mountain breeze. . . . He shook himself, mentally. 'I can't be hunting a man down, Joe. It's not my line of work. I've learned that,' he said, sparing a glance at the sleeping form of John Bass.

'Maybe when you're feeling better,' Joe Adderly said. He rose to answer a tap on the door and let Doctor Sean Leitner in. The physician looked shaky. His white hair was unbrushed. His eyes were reddish and his manner irritable.

'What now, Adderly! I had just fallen asleep.'

'This man is injured,' Adderly said, nodding at Tom Dyce. 'And I've another in the cell with a gunshot wound and a broken wrist.'

'See to Bass first; I'll wait,' Tom said. Now that help was here, it didn't seem so urgent. He knew for certain that he didn't want John Bass to succumb to his bullet wound. Any inquiry into the cause of his demise might take days, delaying Tom's departure, and he meant to be riding north as soon as possible.

The doctor and the marshal were sparring verbally as Adderly took the key to the cell from the rack behind his desk.

'I don't suppose this is a cash call,' Leitner said crossly.

'Prisoners' injuries are paid for by the town, Sean, you know that.'

'It only takes them a month to pay up their bill. Doesn't anyone realize that doctors, like anyone else, have bills to pay and mouths to feed?'

'Take it up with the mayor,' Adderly said, unlocking John Bass's cell.

'What about the other one?' Leitner demanded, not through with his bickering yet. He nodded toward Tom Dyce. 'Cash?'

Adderly's expression grew impatient. 'He's a deputy, Sean. The town pays his doctor bills as well; you know that.' He turned the brass key in the lock and swung the cell door open. John Bass grunted and moved a little on his cot.

The doctor hesitated when he saw who it was.

'That's a dangerous man, Joe. I'll need you to stand by while I treat him.'

After some prodding and poking and a lot of bandaging while the marshal stood by, gun in hand, Leitner announced that he was finished with the man. John Bass flopped back on his cot and fell into a drunken sleep again. The doctor came out to see to Tom's wounds. When he was finished binding Tom's ribs he gave him some advice.

'You are going to have to spend some time in bed, young man. If a cracked rib breaks free, it can do a lot of damage internally. Just forget about any duties you might have for now.'

Dismayed, Tom said, 'I was planning on riding out tomorrow.'

'Jolting around on horseback is probably the worst risk you could take,' Leitner said, placing a not unfriendly hand on Tom's bare shoulder. 'Put off your plans. Whatever they are they can wait a few days. Go home, get some rest. I'll give you something to ease the pain and help you sleep.'

The powder the doctor gave him did help Tom's aching ribs and they did help him to sleep. By midnight he was dead to the world in his hotel room. Unfortunately the medication did nothing to keep him from dreaming, and when he awoke at dawn it was with a lingering dream of the Thibido and Aurora Tyne still in his feverish mind.

TWO

Tom Dyce woke up early. He began from force of habit to swing his feet to the floor, but his body resisted. The pain in his ribs was savage in its determination. He could not go back to sleep and so he lay on the thin mattress, watching the morning shadows move across the room as the sun rose higher. Flat on his back, he watched a spider in a corner of the ceiling spin an intricate web. Restlessly he fought sleep and finally embraced it. What else was there to do?

The doctor came by some time past noon. He examined Tom Dyce's bandages, gave him another paper holding the pain-alleviating powder and went away. Tom took the medicine, yawned widely and lay back waiting for the pain-killer to take effect. The spider's handiwork was lost in shadow now, so there was not even that to amuse him.

He had never yearned so much to be riding the long trail. Memory of all of the discomfort it involved had been softened by time or by the pain-killer. He thought fondly of the open country, not dwelling upon – barely remembering – the days without food or water, the nights spent in the wild with only a thin blanket as protection against the chill of the desert. He did not forget, however, the reason he longed to be up and riding again. He continued to visualize the soft dark hair, the laughing eyes of Aurora Tyne. As with the desert, he managed to set aside in thought the pain her coldness had brought to him. The pain . . . and now as his physical pain diminished he managed to drift away into a land fitted with soft pink clouds. It was a pretty, perfect land without scorn or pain. Tom Dyce was content to be folded into its softness.

Morning arrived with a glare of yellow sunlight beaming through the hotel window and a persistent rattling of the door to his room. Tom regretted being brought back from his life of peace among the clouds. The morning brought a return of pain, although it was somewhat muted now. And, as his stomach reminded him painfully, he was starved. He had eaten nothing at all for a long time. His dreams were vanished and his head had begun to throb again. The rapping at the door continued. He cursed whoever it was for having brought him back to an unhappy reality.

Angrily he yelled, 'Come in!'

The door swung open and Tom saw the apologetic face of Joe Adderly in the gap. There was someone with the thin, red-haired man, but Tom could not make him out, except to see that he wore a sheriff's star.

'All right to come in, Tom?' Adderly asked.

'Might as well, the damage is done,' Tom replied.

Adderly, obviously not understanding Tom's tone or his words, eased into the room. Behind him the hallway door opened wide and a broad-shouldered, heavy-bellied man tramped in. Tom knew who it had to be and a fair idea of what he wanted from him.

'Tom,' Adderly said, removing his hat which he tossed on the bedside table. 'This is Sheriff Harley Griffin out of Ruidoso. He wanted to have a brief talk with you – if you're up to it.'

'I suppose I am,' Tom replied. 'Although my head is still a little fuzzy.'

Griffin, a grim-looking man, pulled up a chair without removing his hat and sat studying Tom speculatively. 'The big man beat you up pretty good, didn't he?' Griffin said.

'Yeah, but he's the one in jail,' Tom said defensively.

'That's what I mean,' Joe Adderly said. 'That's what I told you, Harley. The kid's got what it takes. He sticks to his job.'

Tom had a bad feeling about the direction this conversation was taking. 'You aren't here about this Vance Wynn business, are you? Because I already told you to leave me out of that.'

'You could at least listen to Sheriff Griffin here,' Joe Adderly said, his face assuming a sorrowful expression as if Tom were a child not behaving in front of a guest.

'All right,' Tom said, not quite sighing. With difficulty he sat up in bed, rearranging his pillow as a bolster. 'First,' he said as his stomach again reminded him, of certain needs, 'I would like some coffee and something – anything – to eat. Sandwiches, eggs, soup, I don't care.'

'Already taken care of,' Adderly said with a smile. 'I figured you'd be hungry. I ordered some food on the way up. It should be here soon. So can we talk?'

Tom nodded with resignation. 'We can talk.' All three men glanced toward the door just then as a boy with a tray knocked. He delivered Tom Dyce's breakfast/lunch silently and slipped out. Tom snatched up a ham sandwich from the tray eagerly. 'I can talk and eat at the same time if no one's offended,' Tom said.

'Go ahead,' Sheriff Griffin said, seating himself at the foot of Tom's bed. 'I'll be doing most of the talking anyway, I expect.' The big man sighed, and removed his hat to rub vigorously at his thick, silver-frosted dark hair. He settled his dark eyes on Tom and began.

'Vance Wynn is a nasty piece of work. He's slippery and he's sly. He took the bank in Ruidoso alone, which also means he's reckless. If you read the Wanted poster, you saw that he's a little over average in size – five feet ten, weighs about a hundred and seventy-five pounds.'

Which was close to Tom Dyce's own size, although he hadn't been officially weighed since the day he was born. Sheriff Griffin went on, his voice growing heavy, melancholy.

'He's more – he's a woman-killer. While he was making his escape, he stopped by a ranch house to water and rest his mount and to find whatever grub he could for his run. There was a woman home alone there at the time ... he killed her before leaving.'

The sheriff seemed unable to go on. He closed his eyes tightly and a few tears leaked from the hardened lawman's eyes. Joe Adderly said quietly:

'She was Harley Griffin's wife, Tom.'

Tom paused in his eating, nodding understanding. So that was what Griffin was doing so far from his home county. Tom Dyce couldn't blame the man for wanting Vance Wynn tracked down and hanged, but Tom was still unwilling to make it his own business, sympathy aside.

'The man's gotten away with the town's money, Dyce. We sent out posses in every direction, but we found no trace of him. Then came the word that he had been spotted up near Flagstaff, and I decided to make the ride myself, no matter that I was leaving my county at the worst possible time – I think Joe told you, we've got a range war brewing, and it is going to get ugly.'

'He mentioned it,' Tom said, reaching for the cup of coffee on his tray.

'I cannot let that get out of hand. I took an oath of office, and personal concerns have to be set

26

aside. A couple of days ago Joe told me that you figured to be riding toward the Flagstaff area and that you had been a good lawman, that you had some guts. That's why I came here – to tell you what kind of man Vance Wynn is, why I want him so badly.'

'I can understand that,' Tom replied. 'but I have had enough of working for the law. I mean to find myself a place up on the Thibido and start again.'

'From scratch?' Sheriff Griffin leaned forward, studying Tom intently. 'What sort of chance do you think you have?' Leaning back again, Griffin spread his hands and took on a reasonable tone. 'Dyce, the reward on Vance Wynn has been set at two thousand five hundred dollars. Do you know how much that is? Don't you realize what you could do with it – a young man trying to start out? I make exactly nine hundred and sixty dollars a year. And that's not bad pay just now, when your average cowhand is still pulling down a dollar a day.

'But to do what you have in mind, which I assume is setting up for ranching, a man needs some start-up capital, and there may not ever be a better chance for you to find it than tracking down Vance Wynn. The county will gladly pay the bounty if you catch him with the bank money. Even without it. . . .' Harley Griffin's voice was taut, his eyes icy. 'I'll make sure you get the reward if the man who killed my wife is wiped off the face of the earth.'

Griffin removed himself from the foot of Tom's bed, planted his hat, and stalked heavily from the room. Tom and Joe Adderly both stared at the door the sheriff had closed behind him.

'The man needs some help, Tom,' Joe Adderly said. 'I think he's near the breaking point. Grief over his wife, the knowledge that he might be letting his people down with a futile pursuit of Vance Wynn . . . the man needs some help.'

'So do we all,' Tom said, finishing his coffee.

'Yes, but as I've been telling you, this is an opportunity for you to pull the two of you back up off the floor.'

Tom was quiet for a minute, closing his eyes against the brilliance of the morning sunlight streaming through the hotel window.

'It's a killing job, Joe, isn't it? That's what Griffin really wants – for me to find and kill Vance Wynn?'

'I know you don't like the idea, Tom. It's not in you, but think what a bastard Vance Wynn is. Think of the woman that he killed, the hole in

Harley Griffin's soul. Think how many ordinary lives his taking that money from the Ruidoso bank has ruined. Remember the dreams you're hoping to build on for yourself.'

Tom's eyes were open now, but uncertain. Joe Adderly went on as he rose from his chair:

'I know you don't like the idea, Tom, but maybe it's the only way. Vance Wynn's nothing but a snake. Unpleasant as it can be, in this unsettled country of ours there comes a killing time.'

The new morning was bright. Tom Dyce, saddlebags over his shoulder, stepped out into the yellow light of the day and eased himself down to the street, wanting to see Fog, as his big light gray horse was named, for its coloring and because half the time the animal seemed to be like one of those humans we call lost in a fog. The horse was far from stupid, but it seemed to believe its life was its own and not necessarily tied to any human wishes or ambitions. At times Fog would ease aside as Tom Dyce tried to saddle it, or with seeming inattention take the direction opposite to that suggested by the reins. The gray horse might have tried another man's patience, but Tom was used to him, and knew the horse to be a long-runner, good-tempered and steady despite his occasional moments of rebellion.

Tom hadn't gotten far up the street when he ran into Joe Adderly again. The marshal was standing nervously in the shade of the awning in front of the dry-goods store, his back against a post. He stepped out to meet Tom Dyce in the sunny street.

'Well, Big John Bass is off to territorial prison this morning. I'm waiting for the prison wagon. Want to help me load him up?'

'No,' Tom said shortly. 'I imagine those prison guards are capable of handling men like Bass.'

He started along the street again, stepping aside as a buggy driven by a man in a town suit, accompanied by a lady in green, rolled past, lifting the dust. Adderly fell in beside him. The marshal glanced sideways at Tom and said, 'Sheriff Griffin has headed back to Ruidoso. He had no choice.'

'Fine,' Tom said. He knew that Adderly had further thoughts. They were near the stable before Joe Adderly voiced them.

'Have you given any more consideration to tracking down Vance Wynn, Tom?'

'No. I have no interest in it, Joe.'

'At least take this with you,' Adderly said, handing Tom a folded Wanted poster. 'Who knows, you might come across Wynn in your travels.'

Tom took the poster without comment and tucked it into his shirt pocket. 'I believe I've still got some pay coming to me, Joe,' he said.

'Do you? All right – come by the office before you leave. I'll settle with you there.'

Tom nodded, strode into the dark confines of the stable and whistled sharply. Fog's querying head lifted from the trough and looked out of his stall with dull expectation. He was eager to be out of the pen, but not for a long troublesome ride. The rail-thin stable man, Luke Tanner, came out from the storeroom, blinking at Tom Dyce.

'Hello, Tom. Ready to be moving?'

'Yes, I am.'

Tanner examined Tom speculatively. 'Do you want me to saddle Fog for you? They tell me you got yourself a little beat up.'

'I think I can handle it now, Luke. At least it's time I found out – I'll call you if I need any help.'

'All right,' Tanner replied. 'You know where your tack is.'

The saddle was heavier than Tom remembered, but he swung it onto Fog's back after one false attempt. His cracked ribs were better, but no one could have said they were healed. He was glad he had a patient, lazy horse instead of some young, sleek, feisty mount. Fog accepted his fumbling motions without protest.

Tom paid Tanner for Fog's keep, although rightly it was the town's debt. He led Fog out into the glare of sunshine, squinting up the street toward Adderly's office. He would as soon not see Joe again, but the little bit of back pay he was owed was important to Tom just then.

He wondered as he led Fog that way why the two lawmen – Adderly and Sheriff Griffin – were so eager to have him on Vance Wynn's trail. With Joe, it could be guessed, he was simply too lazy to go hunting the bank robber. Hell, you could also see his point about having the citizens of Rincon to take care of.

But Sheriff Griffin? The bank in Ruidoso had been his responsibility. More – Vance Wynn was said to have killed Harley Griffin's wife. Maybe, Tom thought, he himself was not a normal man. But if some outlaw had killed Tom's wife! He would have ripped off his badge then and there and pursued the murderer to the ends of the earth. But we all don't think the same. After all, Griffin had been chasing the man far out of his home county for a long while. Perhaps he had simply given up, realizing that the people of Ruidoso needed him as well.

Tom shook his head. It didn't matter. He was not a bounty hunter; he was going home to the Thibido range to find out finally if Aurora Tyne cared for him at all, if she would give him another chance.

It was just before noon under a cloudless white sky that Tom, riding the plodding Fog, trailed out of Rincon and pointed his pony's nose northward.

The day held hot and clear, the land was a monotonous stretch of endless miles. There were no landmarks, no trees to be seen. Only the ubiquitous greasewood plants and clumps of nopal cactus which seemed to need no soil, no moisture to survive. Fog walked on at his unenthusiastic pace, and Tom made no attempt to hurry the animal. They plodded onward across the dry land with the molten sun overhead. A stranger on this desolate land might have given up and returned to wherever he had begun his journey, but Tom had passed this way before and he knew that, despite its dismal aspect, there was an end to the journey, that ahead lay water, grass and trees, cool highlands and, just maybe, Aurora Tyne.

Sometime in mid-afternoon Tom glanced to the east and saw a lone rider, or the distant suggestion of a mounted man, for the distance was too great to be sure and heat veils concealed the rider. He frowned. It was a rare and foreign land to travel over unless a man had a very good or desperate reason for doing so. Tom rode on through the afternoon, Fog not growing sluggish, but actually less reluctant to follow the trail into the dry land. Tom had hopes of reaching Coyote Springs on this day – a small, sometimes seasonally dry watering hole he knew of. If they found no water there, he would give Fog water from his canteen to drink in his hat and by morning, both should be strong enough to travel through to the Thibido country.

Or 'Thibideaux'. Tom smiled in remembrance. The first settlers had been vigorously anti-French because of an incident in the northlands many years earlier, and they had voted to change the spelling on the maps to 'Thibido' at a vote of forty-two to one. The only hold-out had been a man named LaFarge. Tom actually laughed at the thought. The smallness of prejudiced minds was universal and a little ridiculous. Although it did make it easier for people to remember how to spell the name.

The rider to Tom's right had drawn much nearer. He was angling toward Tom, had obviously spotted him and intended to move nearer. Tom was not so sure he liked the idea of having a companion along the trail. He liked company, but company he knew. On this open land a man could be shot down and discarded like a cork from a bottle, and as unlikely to ever be found again.

As the sky began to purple in the west Tom came upon what he thought was the Coyote Springs country, but before he could reach it the man who had been riding his way approached, riding a dun-colored horse with flecks of foam on its flanks.

'Howdy!' the stranger called out in a booming voice. Tom, who had unsheathed his Winchester, held up Fog to wait for the man. The stranger struck Tom as an odd proposition. He sat almost sideways in his saddle as if he suffered some affliction, wore a straw hat with a red scarf tied around it as a band, twill trousers and a heavy pair of workboots unsuited for the stirrups. He had a thick black mustache which seemed to leak downward from his nose and cover the corners of his mouth, inquisitive blue eyes and a scar which seemed to cleave his chin. His sun-faded shirt was misbuttoned.

'Hold up, if you don't mind. I think I've lost my way,' he called to Tom.

Tom waited while the man approached. What else was there to do? If the man had truly lost his way on the high desert, to refuse help was the same as sentencing him to death. The shadows beneath the horses grew long as the sun seemed to laze away in the west, leaving a few scattered pennants of pink clouds.

'Do you happen to know where there's water to be found?' the man on the dun horse asked first. Up closer now, Tom could see that the man was suffering some deprivation. Tom handed over his canteen, all the while keeping a close eye on the stranger. The man drank, drank again, nodded his appreciation and handed the canteen back.

'My name is Tarquinian Stottlemeyer,' the man with the dun horse said, wiping his mouth with the cuff of his shirt.

'Tarquinian? I don't think I've ever heard such a name.'

'My mother was very imaginative.' The stranger laughed. 'You can just call me Jeff – I chose that one for myself. Saves a lot of confusion.'

'I'm Tom Dyce. I guess my mother wasn't quite as imaginative.' The two shook hands as Jeff, as he preferred to be called, asked anxiously:

'Do you know of any water holes around here? I didn't know the country rolled out so long.'

Tom told Jeff about Coyote Springs. 'Sometimes after a high country rain it's filled to overflowing. Other times there's nothing but playa. Baked mud and stands of withered cattails. We'll find out how our luck is running in a few miles. I believe I can see the springs ahead, and I think I saw greenery there.'

'I'm hoping,' Jeff said. He patted the neck of his weary dun. 'I'm afraid I didn't do this old boy any good running him out here. Your horse,' he said, looking at Fog, 'looks like he's not bothered much by it.'

'He's desert-born and bred, and he doesn't extend himself any more than he has to at any time.'

The two men trailed their horses through the twilight toward Coyote Springs. Nearing it, they could see that they were in luck. The cattails stood straight and green; even the dry willows showed signs of new leafing at their tips, and a last ray of sunlight glinted off the pond which was shallow, but certainly held enough water for their horses, enough to refill empty canteens.

With the horses picketed near by they rolled out their beds. Tom placed his own bedroll a little away from Jeff's, still not knowing the man at all. Jeff was carrying no food of any kind, so Tom shared a tin of salt biscuits he had purchased before leaving Rincon.

'I thank you,' Jeff said, chewing slowly, drinking much water afterward. 'My stomach thanks you. If I hadn't run into you, I don't know if I could have made it.'

'Where is it you're riding?' Tom Dyce asked, studying the first few stars that had twinkled on to scatter their light across the face of the pond. Something animal moved in the reeds, then splashed into the water. He glanced that way but saw nothing.

'I'm heading up to the Thibido country, hoping to find some work. I hear it's nice up that way.'

'It's not for everybody,' Tom told him. 'It's pretty wild country, but at least it's cooler than it is out here on the flats. What kind of work are you looking for, Jeff?'

'Whatever I can land. I'm tired of town living. If I can't find anything, I might have to ride on to Flagstaff, though. I can't go on much longer without money.'

'There's a couple of small towns up along the Thibido,' Tom told him. 'Or they call them that.'

'Small?'

'That's not the word for them – a trading post, a general store and they call themselves a city.'

A cloud of gnats had begun to rise from some hiding place across the pond. Tom drew his scarf up over his mouth and nose to avoid breathing them in. Jeff seemed untroubled by the swarming insects.

'I'd rather work out of town,' Jeff said with a yawn. 'I know that I'm just a little old – borderline for riding herd, branding, and all – but I wouldn't mind some ranch yard-work, if I could find it. I met a man who told me that a couple of small ranches up this way were growing fast. This man told me that he had just ridden down from such a proposition. Seems he didn't get along with the foreman.'

'That happens,' Tom Dyce said. 'Men sometimes just don't mesh, for no particular reason.'

'Oh, there was a reason,' Jeff Stottlemeyer told Tom. 'He found that the foreman was busy nights using a hot cinch-iron to change the brands on calves.'

'It's been known to happen,' Tom admitted.

'But not usually by the foreman the owner has put into a position of trust.'

'No, I know that,' Jeff said, stretching out in his bed. 'The dirty thing about the whole scheme is that the owner of the ranch is a woman. Can you beat that! Doesn't seem right to rob a woman who's taken a man in and given him the responsibility of watching over her affairs.'

'No, it doesn't,' Tom agreed. He was thinking of many things at once. He laid his head back and asked quietly. 'Do you happen to know the name of the woman?'

'Not for sure. It kinda slipped my mind, but I think the man I met told me it was . . . Ryan, Pine . . . something like that. I only remember that she had a real pretty first name – those being a specialty of mine,' Jeff answered with an unseen smile. 'Aurora, that was it! That's a pretty name, now, isn't it?'

Yes, it was. Not as pretty as Aurora Tyne herself was, however. If she no longer had feelings for Tom, he wished to know. If someone was cheating her, stealing her inheritance, she was going to find Tom around her whether she liked it or not.

THREE

The dawn light purpled the flanks of the hills as they approached them. Here and there the glint of sun-gold limned the peaks brilliantly. The canyons were dark with cool shadow. Jeff anxiously studied the hills which rose to some 4,000 feet.

'I hope my poor pony can make the climb,' he said, removing his straw hat to wipe his brow.

'The trail is nowhere as steep as it looks,' Tom told him confidently. 'It sort of zigzags this way and that toward that saddleback to the west. From then on, it's easy riding. We'll be over the ridge before noon. Then we'll call a halt to it at Flapjack – assuming the wind hasn't blown it away.'

'Flapjack?' Jeff said in puzzlement.

'One of those little settlements I mentioned. It's

41

not much, but they'll have grub for us and hay for the horses.'

'That's all we need for the time being,' Jeff replied. He shrugged sadly, 'Although I can't afford either at the moment.'

'I can let you have a few dollars,' Tom offered.

'I'd appreciate it. You know I'll pay you back as soon as I find myself a situation. . . .' Jeff rambled on, but Tom was uneasy hearing his effusive gratitude. He was no longer listening, but only watching the trail and the uplands as they rode higher, following the wandering path.

Here and there they now began to see pine trees and cedars scattered across the rugged flanks of the hills, and as they crested the saddleback they were met by a cool breeze which chilled their sweat-soaked bodies. They paused to look out across the land and to let the horses blow. Farther along, miles farther, true mountain peaks lifted their heads toward the long sky. They wound their way down to the broad pale-green flats below and, true to Tom's prediction, came upon Flapjack shortly after noon.

'That's it, is it?' Jeff Stottlemeyer asked as they halted again on a low ridge overlooking the valley where Flapjack rested like a wounded creature sagging against the earth. Low, virtually without paint and doomed, it was still a cheering sight, as any such outpost is to a man long on the empty land.

'It is, and believe it or not, it's grown since I saw it last,' Tom said, for he could count nine buildings huddled together along Thibido Creek which was the only justification for Flapjack's existence. Available water played a large part in settlers deciding where they might stop, decide to stay. The first pioneers had their choice of remaining here or trekking more endless miles across the sere desert. Rightly or wrongly they had decided that this was as far as they wished to go – perhaps as far as they could make it.

'What's that one large building, painted yellow?' Jeff asked as they neared the town.

Tom laughed. 'Take your best guess – that's the saloon, of course.' The saloons were the first structures built in a frontier town, and likely to be the only ones that prospered.

'I don't have any interest in drinking or gambling,' Jeff said, 'even if I could afford to do so. But, I'll tell you, Tom, a piece of meat would sure set me up right now.'

'We'll find us some steak and potatoes,' Tom

43

agreed. 'There's two ranches near by, and so beef is not a problem.'

'The Tyne ranch, the one that woman runs?' Jeff said, looking a question at Tom.

'And Art Royal's Circle R. Art's a tough cookie, but he's a good enough man. Maybe he can set you up with something in the way of a job.'

'I can only hope that one of the ranches will take me on,' Jeff said, huffing through his heavy black mustache. 'I can't tell you how bad I need work.'

Tom didn't answer. For reasons he didn't fully understand he had been trying to steer Jeff toward the Circle R, keeping him away from Aurora's Rafter T ranch. He was thinking that he would have enough on his mind without Jeff tagging along, especially if there was any truth to the rumor that Aurora had hired a thieving foreman. He had helped Jeff out, but he wanted no further responsibility for him.

They found Angel Lopez's stable open and swung down to walk their horses inside. Angel, a short, thick-shouldered man, came out of the back, wiping his hands on a towel. He furrowed his brow, studying Tom.

'I know you, don't I?'

'Tom Dyce, Angel. I've been gone for about a year now.'

'Oh, yes.' Angel's face lit up with a smile and the two men shook hands. 'Tom! And that stupid horse of yours, what's his name?'

'Fog. Don't call him stupid, though, Angel.'

'What, he's going to hear me and feel insulted?'

Tom said nothing else. He was unsure why he had come to Fog's defense anyway. It's just that they had traveled many a trail together. If Fog was indeed stupid, perhaps Tom himself was no smarter. He had never figured out a way to charm Aurora Tyne, after all. Thinking about her again, as he did daily, caused his stomach to tighten. How would he react when he actually saw her again, face to face? Like a babbling idiot, he supposed.

'We'll leave the horses to you, Angel,' Tom said. 'Now, partner,' he said to Jeff, 'let's find us some food.'

'You know Carrie's Kitchen?' Angel suggested. 'Those apple trees that Art Royal planted have started to bear fruit, and Carrie can serve up a good apple pie these days.'

'Thanks, Angel. I know the place. That's where we're going,' Tom said as Angel began stripping the two weary horses of their gear. The stableman only lifted a hand to send them on their way. He was more comfortable with horses than humans, as were many men in his trade.

They walked the street toward the restaurant. Most of the buildings opened directly onto the street; only the saloon seemed prosperous enough to have constructed a porch with an awning which shaded the two wooden benches resting before its bright yellow façade. They could hear men laughing inside the saloon as they passed and someone plucking a badly tuned banjo.

'They start early here, don't they?' Jeff said.

'Most of them don't have anything to do but drink. There's no work to speak of. A lot of men are out of work.'

'Well, they got money for whiskey, don't they?'

'If you're a drinker, that comes first,' Tom said. In passing the saloon they noticed a tall man with a long, fine-pointed mustache wearing an odd combination of buckskin trousers, blue silk shirt and light-blue jacket. His eyes were cool and dangerous-looking. They followed Jeff and Tom Dyce along the street.

'Don't ever get into a card game with that fellow,' Tom said.

'No!' Jeff agreed with a laugh. For both men

had seen the way the stranger wore his gun. There was a holster stitched to his calf-high boot. It seemed an awkward place to wear a Colt – if you were standing up. But if he were sitting across the table from you, he could have that weapon drawn and fired from where it rode long before a man could come to his feet and go for his belt gun.

'Seen that trick before, have you?' Tom asked.

'The gambler's rig? A time or two. Enough so that I know I don't want to sit in on a card game opposite anyone who wears a gun that way. It's designed strictly for killing.'

Tom nodded. They had come to the entrance to Carrie's Kitchen, which was of adobe with narrow slit windows in the front and a plain wooden door to enter by. The restaurant was nothing special to look at, but upon entering they were met with the steamy smells of steaks frying and the almost exotic scent of fresh apple pie. The subtler smells of potatoes boiling and of cabbage were almost as agreeable.

'I'm ready to go from one end of her menu to the other,' Jeff said, removing his straw hat.

'I don't think Carrie's got a menu,' Tom replied. 'You get whatever she has cooking and plenty of it.'

'That suits me fine,' Jeff said agreeably. They

47

found a table not far from the kitchen door and seated themselves. After a while, Carrie – a dumpy sort of asymmetrical woman, with gray-streaked dark hair – came to greet them, her pad poised in her work-roughened hand. Pencil lifted, she stopped and stared at Tom curiously.

'Well, Tom Dyce! You're back. How in the world is Aurora doing?'

'I was about to ask you the same thing,' Tom answered.

'You haven't been out to the ranch yet?'

'Not yet. I don't know what kind of welcome I'll receive.'

'Why wouldn't you be welcome?' Carrie asked.

'No real reason, it's just that things kind of came to a dead end out there for me.'

An impatient, bald man took the table next to them and demanded service. Carrie apologized with her expression and went to see to him.

'You didn't tell me that you knew this Aurora Tyne,' Jeff said. His hat was in his lap, his hands toying with the silverware on the table.

'It didn't seem important.'

'It's just that maybe I said too much about the goings-on up there.'

'It's of no consequence, Jeff. I'm glad you told

me what you did.'

Carrie was back, ready for their orders. 'Some of everything, I suppose,' Tom said, finding that easiest.

'Right, will you be wanting coffee first?'

'If you don't mind.'

'I'll see to that – there she is,' Carrie said, lifting a hand in the direction of a small woman with a mop of red hair, stained apron, bright-blue eyes. The girl held a one-gallon coffee pot, using a towel for a hot pad. 'That's Laura. My niece. She came out to Flapjack for a try at the business, but she doesn't like it much.'

'Not many can stick Flapjack,' Tom said as the girl made her way toward their table. 'People are mostly trying to get out of here. They're even too ashamed to say where they're from. They'll usually just answer with "the Flagstaff area" if you ask them. Who wants to admit to being a Flap-jackian?'

Carrie smiled. 'I know, there's not much to brag about, is there? Still, though the refugees outnum-ber them, we see new faces around here every day. A part of that is the way Aurora Tyne's ranch is booming. I guess she'll be bringing in a record herd this year.'

'I heard they were losing cattle,' Tom said without mentioning Jeff's rumor of rustling.

'I wouldn't know,' Carrie said. 'I'm stuck here in town. I just know what folks tell me, and they tell me the ranch is prospering, since she brought in that new foreman, Ray Fox . . . oh, I'm sorry, Tom, I didn't mean that anyone was saying anything against the way you managed the ranch for Aurora.'

'It's all right,' Tom said. 'As long as she's doing well.'

The bald man at the next table had begun impatiently tapping his fork against his empty plate.

'Sorry, Mr Jefferson,' Carrie said to him. 'I'll take care of you right away.'

'Some of us have work to do, you know,' Jefferson said grumpily.

'Yes, sir. I'm sorry,' Carrie said with a wink at Tom. Then she bustled away toward the kitchen as her young red-headed niece, Laura, arrived with the coffee pot, turned the cups over and filled them.

'Carrie tells me you're tired of Flapjack already,' Tom tried. He had been observing the expression on the young woman's face. It altered quickly from cheery to cloudy, depending, it seemed, on how she was spoken to. He supposed Laura was what they called mercurial: not a desirable trait for a waitress whose job was always to present a happy face to the public.

'I was tired of Flapjack from the day I set foot in it,' Laura said, and now her face was only wistful.

'So, you're leaving?'

'I'm leaving. Saturday. The Overland Stage Company has deigned to provide Flapjack with service – one day a week. They say the traffic doesn't justify more than that, which is a surprise to me – you'd think the people from this town would be stampeding out of here.'

'Different people have different expectations,' Tom said and Laura offered him a bright smile.

'Yes. That's why I'm leaving,' she said, and then, answering a summoning call from the opposite corner, she rushed away.

'Pretty little thing,' Jeff commented as Laura walked away, 'though she seems a little emotional.'

'Just disappointed with her lot in life,' Tom guessed. 'When we're younger we expect everything to turn out the way we imagine it will; it seldom does. How about you, Jeff? What did you imagine yourself doing when you were her age?'

'Distinguishing myself in a couple of wars and

owning a railroad,' Jeff said with a grin. 'Now I haven't two nickels to rub together.'

Carrie had returned from the kitchen, performing an acrobatic act with three platters, one of which she gave the impatient bald man. The other two she placed in front of Tom and Jeff. 'You want any more, you just let me know,' Carrie said.

'If I want anymore after this,' Tom said, 'have me examined as a medical curiosity!' Their platters were heaped with boiled potatoes, buttered cabbage and thick steaks. And they had their apple pie to deal with later.

The two men got to it, not wasting any more time on conversation. From time to time the harassed-appearing Laura would pass their table and Tom could always spare the time to glance at her. He felt sorry for the girl and faintly attracted to her. But Laura carried her shield high. Anyway, all thoughts of another woman would be obliterated the moment he saw Aurora Tyne again. He fell into a brief reverie concerning her tall, slim figure, the dark, shining hair, her constant smile. . . .

'Don't forget to eat,' Jeff Stottlemeyer said, bringing Tom out of his waking dream. What Jeff thought of Tom's inattention was unimportant.

Tom finished the rest of his meal with a sort of resignation, not eagerness. Jeff was already working on his second slab of thick apple pie spiced with cinnamon before Tom placed his fork and knife aside.

'Better try some of this pie,' Jeff advised. 'It's superior!' Jeff dabbed at his curtain-sized black mustache with his napkin and went on eating as Tom rose to find the register. He was suddenly eager to get on out to the Tyne ranch. His uncertainty could no longer be coddled. He needed to ride to the place, find Aurora and discover just how much had changed, and where he stood in the new arrangement.

A Mexican woman Tom had never seen before made change for him with painful slowness, mouthing each cent as she paid out Tom's money. Tom tucked the change away, barely counting it. The amount didn't concern him just then. He still had the cash he had saved and his last month's pay, which Joe Adderly had reluctantly forked over. Reaching into his pocket, Tom's hand brushed against a piece of paper he had nearly forgotten about the wanted poster on the bank robber, Vance Wynn.

The sum offered was $2,500. An incredible

amount of money to be offered for the cost of one .44 caliber round which could take Wynn down. Enough for a man to buy land and stock it with sleek cattle – shorthorns, maybe, even enough to build a small house. . . .

Tom shook his head. What was he thinking of? He was not a man-hunter and would have no idea where to start looking for the elusive Vance Wynn.

As he shuffled back into the restaurant Tom found Jeff Stottlemeyer virtually alone in the room, finishing off a last cup of coffee.

'Ready?' Tom asked. Jeff looked at him with subtle pleasure.

'I'm not going to be going anywhere, Tom. I know you don't really want me trailing with you, anyway.' He waved off Tom's denial and continued. 'You know that man at the next table, Mr Jefferson? Guess what – he owns the Foothill Saloon. I told him I was looking for a position and he offered me a job swamping out the place. Free room and reasonable pay. All I have to do is sweep and mop out the place, try to clean up any damage from the night before.'

'I thought you didn't want any kind of town work,' Tom said.

'Oh, well, I didn't. But you know, Tom, when you're looking for work, the first offer is the best. Who knows if one of the ranches would even take me on?'

'Well,' Tom said doubtfully, 'I hope it works out for you, Jeff.'

'Working a broom isn't going to kill me, son,' Jeff said, huffing through his mustache. 'It'll be the best situation I've been in for a long time,' he winked, 'and not two blocks away from the best food I've ever eaten.'

Tom laughed. He was happy to shed Jeff, not because he didn't enjoy his company, but because he had no idea what to do with the man. Tom had felt vaguely responsible for Jeff; now he was no longer burdened by that responsibility.

Tom stopped by the kitchen to wave to Carrie and thank her. Against the far wall, one leg drawn up, her arms crossed beneath her breasts, he saw Laura looking out the window as if expecting the stagecoach to take her away from this. She did not glance at Tom. He wished the girl well, but he felt no obligation toward her. She was out in the wild world, let her make the best of it as everyone else did.

For Tom it was time. He would retrieve Fog from

the stable and ride home once more, if home it was. He needed to meet with Aurora Tyne and discover which way his world was tilted.

FOUR

The day remained cool, a slight breeze off the north shifting the boughs of the thick stands of pine. The gray horse Tom Dyce rode moved onward at its usual regular pace. Now and then Fog would lift his head and his ears would prick as if it had some vague memory of the trail they traveled, but then the horse would shake its head and continue. That was Fog: he seemed to have no memory, at least not like that which was often associated with other, smarter horses.

Tom was not blessed with such amnesia. He passed the knoll where wood for the winter had been trimmed back along the verge, saw the lupine-studded vale where he and Aurora had gone for a summer picnic. That was her first attempt at frying chicken for them and, in truth, it wasn't very good, but that hadn't mattered a bit. Nothing could have spoiled that day. Ahead now, Tom caught a glimpse of the green peaked roof of the Tyne house and his heart constricted a little. He felt like running away, giving it up. As he had on the day he had packed his goods and left when Aurora rejected him.

Why, he did not know. It is probably a mistake to revisit our lives and try to discover where things went wrong, but here he was attempting it, trying to convince himself that he must because he had been told – third-hand – that her foreman, Ray Fox, was rustling her cattle. Yet he had also been told that Rafter T was prospering, that Aurora's outlook was bright. His concerns seemed vague and flimsily constructed. He rode on, weaving through the pine forest, head hanging as low as Fog's.

There are few things as pathetic as a jilted lover.

The sky had turned cobalt blue, and there were thunderheads massing over the distant mountains when Tom Dyce guided Fog into the yard of the Tyne ranch where a dozen massive oaks flourished. The big white house Darren Tyne had constructed at vast expense and never lived long enough to enjoy fully stood basking in the rays of late sunlight. A yard dog came out from beneath the house, barking at the strange rider and horse.

The front door swung open and Aurora Tyne emerged to stand in the late sunlight, glowing as if her beauty had drawn the golden rays to her for that purpose. Tom was struck dumb, feeling the absolute fool as, at the same time, he thought he had stumbled upon an ancient, hoped-for, but undiscoverable temple.

She smiled. She wore an off-purple sort of dress Tom could not find a name for, a narrow gold necklace and had her dark hair pinned up in an intricate arrangement. It seemed she had been waiting for someone – certainly not the trail-dusty Tom Dyce. Aurora stepped off the porch, her arms extended.

'Tom!' she cried as if she were truly happy he had returned. Tom swung down wearily and accepted her hands. She offered him a brief kiss on the cheek. It was odd to find cherished memories having form and substance. Should he have folded in her arms, murmured apologies, explanations. . . ? He hadn't the skills for that.

'And Fog! How are you, Foggy? Tom, do you remember the day we were sitting out here on the porch, watching Fog browse his way across the yard, nibbling at the grass. With his head down he walked right into the barn wall! We laughed as he backed off and shook his head in surprise. Poor old Fog,' she said, stroking the gray's neck and muzzle. 'You've always been a sweet, confused old creature.'

Which made him a match for his owner, Tom thought.

'You're all dressed up this evening,' Tom said, fumbling his way through small talk.

'Yes,' Aurora answered brightly. 'I like Ray to have a pleasant place to come back to after a hard day's work.'

'Ray Fox?'

'Yes, do you know him?'

'People in town mentioned his name,' Tom said.

'He's doing wonders out here. Tom, Ray is a good, hard-working man, and I guess you know that I think a lot of him.'

'I guessed as much,' Tom admitted.

'I know that once,' she said softly, taking his hands again, 'we thought there might be a future for us. But this is different, Tom. I want Ray for my man.'

Tom Dyce felt his heart sink, but why had he

expected anything else? He had been gone long from the ranch. 'I wonder why sometimes, that's all,' he said numbly.

'Oh, I don't know, Tom,' Aurora replied. 'After Father died I had so much on my mind that I couldn't think of anything but making a go of the ranch. It was the timing more than anything else,' she said gently, perhaps trying to soften his obvious pain. 'And there are times when a woman does not need a man, others when she almost aches for one.' Her dark eyes were soft and penetrating. 'There's no way of telling when the emotions will rise to that level. It was just too soon for me then, Tom.'

'And now it's too late for me,' he said dismally although he smiled faintly. Behind him he heard the arrival of a horse, and Aurora looked over his shoulder.

'Oh, here's Ray now.' The light in her eyes changed, brightened. Looking again at Tom, she said seriously, 'I want you two to be friends, Tom. Ray is a good man. I want you to get to know him – for my sake.'

While Aurora was cooking supper in the kitchen the two men sat in front of a low fire burning in the huge stone fireplace. Tom and Ray Fox spoke together, Tom uneasily. Tom was taken by the face and form, the affability of the Rafter T's new foreman. He was also struck by Ray Fox's resemblance to the description on the Wanted poster for Vance Wynn. That was stretching things, he realized. The man could not be Vance Wynn. Or could he? Why not? Fox had appeared in the region at about the time the bank in Ruidoso was held up, and he knew Sheriff Harley Griffin, as was made clear during their conversation.

'Yes, I knew the old coot when I was working the Ruidoso Basin. I can't say we exactly got along, though,' Ray Fox answered when Tom mentioned the name.

Tom was letting jealousy and his imagination run away with him, he knew. Still, he shook his head. The only way he could ever be sure was by way of a concealed clue that Vance Wynn carried. The robber had once been in a shoot-out down in El Paso and bore a spider-shaped scar on the small of his back, according to the poster which Tom had studied many times by now. He could hardly ask Fox to yank up his shirt and prove he was not a criminal.

And what if Fox was that criminal, Vance Wynn? Would Tom be helping Aurora or destroying her hopes for the future by revealing it?

The fire burned lower and Aurora called them to supper. Tom let his suspicions fade away during the course of the meal. It was painful to watch Aurora's cheerful face, the way she never got up from the table or returned to it without letting her hand brush across Ray Fox's shoulder, but she was obviously happy, as was Fox. Was it because Fox had found himself in a lucky position – a lovely orphan woman and a prosperous ranch his for the taking, or was it deeper, more real?

Tom once again felt ashamed of himself. Ray Fox was speaking: 'If you are meaning to hire on and stay around for a while, Tom, you can start tonight, if you're up to it after your long ride. We've been having a lot of trouble with cut wire up along the boundary with the Circle R. Someone's been making off with unbranded calves, and we can't afford to lose those dogies.

'You probably know that country better than most of the men we have on hand – they're mostly new-hires. If you'd feel up to making a patrol of the north fence, it would be a help. Me,' he went on stretching his long arms, 'I've about had it for today. I've got to get some sleep.'

Ray Fox rose then, kissed Aurora on the cheek,

and headed for the stairs, surprising Tom, who had expected the foreman to head toward the bunkhouse, leaving himself and Aurora alone to continue their interrupted conversation.

Aurora, clearing the table, said with her eyes turned down, 'Ray has Father's room now. It made no sense to leave it empty.'

'How about one more cup of coffee?' was what Tom replied.

In truth Tom was too tired to be riding fence that night, but his excited thoughts kept him awake and alert. He had found out that Aurora loved another man who, he suspected, was a bank robber as well as a cattle thief. What now? He couldn't go off half-cocked and accuse Fox baselessly. Nor could he let Ray get away with it if it was true.

Riding Fog, he made his way to the north fence line, which as Ray had noted, Tom did know better than any recently hired man could. He and Darren Tyne, Loco Steve, Pat and the other old hands had strung the wire over the rocky ground, down into the ravines and up again one grueling-hot summer a few years ago. Aurora used to ride out to bring her father and the hands cool water. . . .

Again Tom found himself thinking about the past, unwilling to let it go, knowing that it was of no use to continue dwelling on it.

The moon rose early, but it was a pitiful gray moon tinged with only a small arc of gold, casting barely enough light to lessen the silver sparkle of the stars. The night was cool and clear, the woodland creatures stirring. Tom guided Fog along the fence line, at times wondering why he had agreed to the job, had not just turned tail and gone.

He knew the answer to that even if he could not admit it. Why continue to pursue a woman who had found her man? But what if that man was of the criminal sort, meaning only to get his grasping hands on the ranch? Tom's head swam with the many ramifications. If Ray Fox had a bag full of money stolen in Ruidoso, he did not need the ranch. If he did not have the bag, then he was not Vance Wynn, but a totally innocent man who meant only to help Aurora.

At the hour before midnight Tom came upon a place where the fence wire had been cut. It was on the edge of a shallow valley along a trail which would have been the natural path for cattle to wander were the fence not there. Ahead of him and half-surrounding him, there was a curtain of dark pine trees. The wind was chill now, and Tom hunched his shoulders as he tried to read the sign on the soft dark earth. Cattle, yes. Horses as well, but nothing to place the two together. Some of the cattle had been very young, judging by the sign, and that was what rustlers would be looking for at this time of year – unbranded calves. Tom eased through the fence and made his way northward, trying to distinguish the horses' hoofprints in the shallow glow of the moon. Someone was up to something, that was for sure. Who, he could not guess from the faint clues.

The first rifle shot was so near that it spanged off the pommel of his saddle, the second tagged Tom in the shoulder and sent him reeling. He hit the grassy earth hard, landing on his injured shoulder as the echoes slowly died away in the dark, forested distance. Tom tried to claw at his Colt, to drag it from his holster for protection. Lying on his injured shoulder, he found it impossible and he could only lie against the cold ground and wait as the pounding hoofs of approaching horses drove down upon him.

'Well, we got him,' one of the men on horseback said from out of the darkness.

'At least one of them,' another voice agreed.

'What do you want to do, Cory? Finish him off, string him up?'

A small light in the back of Tom's mind flickered on and he managed to groan: 'Cory? Cory Stamps?'

There was a confused silence then, followed by a man's grunt as he swung down from the saddle and walked to where Tom lay. The man bent down and whistled. 'It's Tom Dyce,' he told the others.

'Dyce? What the hell. . . ?' A second man swung down from leather and approached Tom.

'Tom, it's Wade Block. What in the world are you doing out here!'

Block and Cory Stamps were both Circle R riders; Tom had known them as neighbors for years. They pulled him to his feet and let him lean against Fog for support. 'Tom,' Wade Block, a man built like his name, apologized, 'we would never have fired had we known it was you. It's just that there's been so much trouble going on out here – calves being poached and some found with suspicious brands. We—'

'It's all right,' Tom said shakily. The fall from his horse had started his ribs aching again, and the bullet through his shoulder caused it to burn fiercely. 'I just am in need of some help right now.'

'Mr Royal's house is closer,' Block said to Cory Stamps. 'Besides, it ain't safe for us to ride onto Rafter T just now.'

Cory Stamps agreed and the three of them lifted Tom onto Fog's patient back. Then they assisted him to make his way to the Circle R, half a mile across the long valley, as the moon rose higher.

Tom had no real memory of the evening. He was prodded and bandaged and given hot drinks and shuffled off into a bed with clean sheets inside the large Circle R log ranch house. In the morning bright sunlight brought him awake. The silhouette of a man in a chair slowly took on form and Tom recognized the old man with the silver mustache, his hair parted in the middle and slicked back.

'Art,' Tom managed to say around an encrusted tongue.

'It's me, son,' Art Royal replied. 'Want a little water?' Tom nodded. 'What in the world were you doing out on Circle R range last night – I know you weren't rustling. Not you.'

'They sent me out, Art,' Tom said, accepting a sip of water from the glass in Art Royal's gnarled hands. He laid his head back. 'Or, at least, Ray Fox did. He said that the wire had been cut and the Rafter T was losing cattle.'

'That's oppositely true,' Art said. 'The wire *has* been cut, but I'm the one losing cattle, not the Rafter T. Fox should know that, and he definitely knows that I have given my hands permission to shoot if any Rafter T men are seen on my side of the wire. He gave you a dangerous job, Tom, and he has to have known it.'

'I suppose so,' Tom said quietly, taking another drink of well water.

'Why, then, would you do it? Being a man of at least normal intelligence?' Art frowned. 'Oh. I know – Aurora could ask you to leap through fire in a camp full of Paiutes and you'd probably do it.'

'Aurora didn't ask me to do it,' Tom said defensively.

'All right – I'm sorry I said that. What happened between you two, Tom? And why are you back?'

'What happened? She didn't love me, Art. Now she thinks she loves Ray Fox.'

'Does she?'

'I don't know. That's why I'm back – a part of it. I wanted to know if she was doing all right. . . .'

'Without you?' the older man asked.

'Yes. I thought she might have changed her

mind after a year. I thought maybe this Ray Fox was not the sort of man she needed . . . oh, hell Art, I don't know what I thought!'

Art stood up and smiled. 'Just take it easy for now. Want me to send a rider over there to tell her what happened? It's daylight now and it should be safe enough. Aurora will be worried.'

'Let her worry!' Tom said with unexpected force. 'No, don't send a man, Art. I wouldn't want someone else to risk his life for me. I didn't know that this had become a shooting war. What happened to the way it used to be?'

'I don't know exactly,' Art Royal said. 'Darren Tyne and I were always good neighbors. Aurora was everyone's little darling. You were always a man I could deal with over petty squabbles – like the time Pat and Loco Steve. . . .' Art shook his head. 'I don't know what happened, Tom. You said you thought that Ray Fox was not the sort of man Aurora needed around her. Did you mean anything by that? Or is it just personal?'

'I don't know, Art. I truly don't. If you don't mind, I think I could use a little more sleep just now.' He found his mind shutting itself down; it was an effort to form words. His lips felt numb. 'How's Fog?' were the last words he remembered speaking before disappearing again into the too-familiar world of pink clouds.

FIVE

It was a wide circle to skirt the Rafter T, but Fog didn't seem to mind, and Tom was starting to believe that he had learned a lesson about letting himself be drawn into affairs he did not completely understand. He had time to think about it on the long trail.

He and Art Royal had had a long conversation about the funny business taking place in the long valley, and Tom could not believe that Art had anything to do with it. He was missing many calves, he told Tom, 'And you almost have to think it couldn't be someone from outside the valley. Why would they come all the way up here to rustle a few dogies, then just disappear like they have? We haven't been able to track the calves any farther

72

than the fence line. I'm sorry, Tom, but it seems as if someone from the Rafter T has to be involved in this.'

Which lent support to the tales Jeff Stottlemeyer had heard.

What then? Ride back to the Rafter T and accuse Ray Fox of stealing cattle in front of Aurora, who believed that her foreman could do no wrong? What would that profit Tom himself? Nothing, except to lower Aurora's estimation of him. Besides, Tom knew he was in no shape for a fight, which would likely be Fox's reaction to any such accusation – the truth of which Tom had no proof at all. He could also accuse the foreman of actually being the robber Vance Wynn, demand that he remove his shirt to prove that he had a spider-shaped scar there. And if he did not? Tom felt boxed into a corner where the only result could be his humiliation and loss of favor in Aurora's eyes.

Brooding, Tom Dyce rode the long trail up Split Mountain and angled his horse toward the flats below. Like it or not, he was going to have to pay another visit to the doctor, if one, or someone resembling one could be found in Flapjack. The last one Tom could remember was a young physician with wild straw-colored hair named Coughlin. He had lasted almost a month in Flapjack. Wade Block had done as well as he could on Tom's shoulder wound, swabbing it with carbolic and stitching it up roughly, but Wade was no doctor. Tom thought that there might even be a fragment of lead remaining in the wound. Whatever the reason, his shoulder was swollen, inflamed and aching. It obviously needed some attention.

Fog dragged his hoofs along the empty main street of Flapjack as the sun began its lazy tilt toward the west. It was hot, dry. Tom made for Carrie's Kitchen, in search of food and liquid. The first person he saw on alighting from Fog was Jeff Stottlemeyer, who was emerging from the restaurant. Jeff wore new jeans and a new green shirt, though his old straw hat was in place. He smiled at Tom, noticing his ripped shirt and pallid face.

'Well, well, old friend,' Jeff said approaching with his hand out. 'It looks like you've done some hard riding since I last saw you.'

Tom took his hand warmly. 'You could say that – I got myself winged putting my nose into other people's business.'

'That's always a bad idea,' Jeff agreed. He was squinting away the sunlight which touched his eyes despite the low-tugged hat he wore. 'The woman's trouble was it? That Miss Aurora you talk about?'

'That's it, Jeff. I thought I was going to ride in and solve something – I didn't, I just got myself near killed.'

'Well,' Jeff said not unsympathetically, 'that seems to be the way it always goes – especially with a woman involved in your decision-making.'

'I guess so,' Tom said reluctantly. 'Say, Jeff, you've been around and about, listening to talk. Is there any sort of doctor in Flapjack these days?'

'No,' Jeff wagged his head, 'not that I've heard of. Though this town sure could use one, the way they are bent on shooting each other up.'

'Oh? Has there been trouble?'

'At the Foothill saloon last night, only a few hours after I got settled in. Over a gambling debt – that's no surprise! No one ever believes he has lost and has to actually pay off the man who won. That's one reason I don't gamble myself.'

'Who was it? Anyone I know?' Tom asked.

'I'm not sure, Tom. The man who done the killing was Lee Tremaine. You seen him but never were properly introduced – the man who wears a pistol stitched to his boot.' Tom remembered the tall man with the pointed mustache and cold eyes well enough; he had struck both him and Jeff as a dangerous man to deal with.

'The subject was a trailsman from down south. Had too much to drink and too little to spend. Upshot was, he challenged Lee Tremaine, and we both know that was a bad idea. Tremaine shot him from where he sat as the stranger tried to rise and grab for his pistol.'

Jeff continued, 'You know, Tom, Tremaine isn't such a bad sort. He even offered to pay for the stranger's funeral. I've heard some talk around town this morning that a few of the more substantial citizens are saying it's time for a change. They're even thinking about finding a marshal for Flapjack. Tom, you—'

'I haven't any interest,' Tom Dyce said firmly. 'I'm through with all of that.'

'Don't get angry,' Jeff replied. 'It's just that I know you have some experience and don't have a situation right now. I sort of mentioned your name to Mr Jefferson and a few of the men in town. Most of them know you from other times, of course. The job is yours for the taking.'

'No, thanks,' Tom said, making his way toward Carrie's door. 'I'm not interested.'

'There is one other thing,' Jeff persisted.

'What's that?'

'Some people were talking – they have the idea that the man Lee Tremaine shot was really Vance Wynn.'

Carrie's Kitchen was close, smoky, already familiar. Tom eased himself down on a chair at a corner table. Carrie approached him with concern in her eyes.

'Now what have you done, Tom?'

'What do you mean?'

'I was watching you from across the room. You looked like an old invalid trying to settle your bones into that chair.' She was studying the ripped shirt, seeing the bandaging beneath it on his shoulder. 'You're just a glutton for punishment, aren't you?' she scolded.

'I suppose,' Tom said wearily. The pain in his shoulder had began to flare up violently. His ribs were still protesting their abuse. Tom lowered his face to his hands.

'You'd know, Carrie: is there anyone around who pretends to be a doctor?'

'Only Laura,' Carrie answered. 'She was studying to be a nurse for a year or so before she ran out of money and had to come out here.'

'I wonder if she'd look at my shoulder?'

'I don't know. I imagine so. Meantime, what can I get you, Tom?'

'Water? Coffee? Maybe a slab of apple pie.'

'Coming right up,' she said, resting a hand on Tom's good shoulder. Then she waddled away toward another table.

Tom kept his face buried in his hands, his eyes shut tightly. When the rustling of garments caused him to open them again, it was to find Laura at his table with a coffee pot and a wedge of cinnamon-spiced apple pie. The young red-haired girl with the changeable aspect was smiling just now, showing even rows of pearl-white teeth.

'Coffee?' she asked.

'Sure.' Tom kept his eyes down as Laura poured.

She said: 'I'm sorry I was in a grouch the other day when I talked to you.'

'No need to apologize,' Tom said. 'We all have our bad moments.'

'It's just that I'm usually not like that. I let things get to me sometimes.'

'What's changed?' Tom asked, sipping at his hot coffee.

'Nothing! Just the page of my calendar. Why, it's Thursday already.'

'And you're still planning on leaving on the Saturday stagecoach?'

'That I am,' she said positively.

'Any idea where you're heading?'

'Well, first to Rincon, I guess. That's where the stage makes its next stop. I understand that I might have to lie over there for a day. Do you know Rincon?'

'Quite well,' Tom told her. 'I was deputy marshal there for a while.'

Laura's eyes had changed. Tom saw her studying his badly bandaged arm through the tear in his sleeve. 'That doesn't look good,' she said. Tom had forgotten that Laura had studied nursing. 'Those red streaks creeping down your arm. How was it treated?'

'Range style – rough stitching and a lot of carbolic.'

'You'd better let me have a look at it – after work. I get off at four o'clock. I have one of the little cottages out back of the restaurant: Cabin C.'

'I wouldn't want to trouble you,' Tom said.

'It's no trouble,' Laura said cheerfully. 'Maybe it will get me back in the frame of mind to resume my nursing studies.'

'That's what you plan on doing?'

'It is. That's about all I ever wanted to do.'

With that she was gone, walking to another table where an old-time prospector was gesturing for more coffee. Probably his first restaurant coffee in months. Tom had tried prospecting, too, summoned by news of a gold strike. He didn't care for perching on mountain tops for day after day, panning in icy water for dust that wasn't enough to pay for his next grubstake.

What was he going to do, he wondered? Everyone else had plans: Laura and her nursing; Aurora and her growing ranch. Jeff, Ray Fox, Art Royal – they all had plans. Tom hadn't an idea. He could, he supposed, take the opening for the new town marshal of Flapjack, but was that really gaining him any ground? He rose and left the restaurant, paying the same painfully slow Mexican cashier.

There was still a great deal of sunlight left when Tom walked out into the day. His shoulder ached, his ribs ached. The light of the sun caused an ache behind his eyes. He stopped the first man he saw.

'Can you tell me who does the mortician's work in town?'

'Are you planning on needing one?' the stranger asked with a half-smile.

'Not just yet. Can you tell me, please?'

The man removed his hat and scratched at his head. 'These days it seems to me that Bridgeport, the blacksmith, is taking care of those things. You might try his place.'

Tom thanked the man and walked away. He knew where the blacksmith's had been, although he had never heard the name Bridgeport before. Flapjack continued to change. There were few familiar faces to be seen around town.

Tom found the smith at his forge, his forehead beaded with sweat. He walked through the shed, and the smith turned as Tom introduced himself. The blacksmith wiped his hand on the front of his leather apron and shook hands with him.

Bridgeport was a short, wiry man who had muscles in his arms that looked as if he had forged them himself. That sort of work has a way of shaping a man – and of wearing him out quickly. 'I understand you are attending to burials these days.'

'As a sideline,' Bridgeport said with distaste. 'A man does what he can to make a few extra dollars.'

'Yes, well I wanted to see the body of the man who was killed in the Foothill saloon last night – if you haven't planted him yet.' At Bridgeport's uncertain look, Tom embellished a little. 'I'm a deputy marshal out of Rincon. I think I might be able to identify him. And if it is him, he was a wanted fugitive. There could even be some reward money attached to him.'

'Is that so?' the blacksmith said, placing his tongs aside. 'I'm not the one who got him, you know?'

'I know – that was Lee Tremaine, I've been told.'

'So they are saying,' Bridgeport answered carefully.

'No one's in any trouble about the killing,' Tom assured him. 'It's just that if he's my man I can quit chasing him and go home.'

'I understand. He's in the back – it's cooler there. I was planning on digging a hole for him near sundown. Come on; I'll show you.'

Tom followed Bridgeport to the rear of the building which held half a dozen horses waiting for new shoes, and unfinished projects of iron, a plow and metal hitch rail included. There was slag underfoot everywhere. Bridgeport might have been a fine craftsman, but he was a slovenly housekeeper. They came to an unlocked side door, no larger than a pantry and Bridgeport gestured.

'There he is. Tremaine . . . whoever it was . . . got

him right through the heart,' Bridgeport stuttered. It was obvious that Bridgeport didn't want to get involved in legalities or get on Lee Tremaine's bad side.

'Thanks,' Tom said. He had no interest at all in Lee Tremaine's legal position. He only wanted to know if this, as Jeff had suggested, was Vance Wynn. Of similar height and weight, he might have been. The waxen figure had lost all resemblance to a human being. Tom noticed that the man's boots were missing, but said nothing. As Bridgeport had said, a man does what he can to make a few extra dollars.

It wasn't Vance Wynn.

Tom lifted the body by the hip and searched for but did not discover the spider-shaped scar the robber was reported to have on the small of his back. He shook his head.

'Not your man?' Bridgeport asked.

'No. I guess I'll just have to keep looking,' Tom said with false unhappiness. He could not have cared less about Vance Wynn, except concerning the man's possible involvement with Aurora Tyne under the identity of Ray Fox. He walked out of the smith's shop as Bridgeport returned to his forge, pumping his bellows with deliberate strength.

Now what?

Tom pondered that as he walked the hot dusty street of Flapjack. His arm was filled with jagged pain, his ribs not much better after all the extra riding he had been doing. If he had any sense, he decided, he would simply leave Flapjack for good and all and quit his probably pointless worrying over Aurora's future. Those range disputes had a way of getting worked out, usually the rough way.

He walked Fog back to Angel Lopez's stable. Whatever he decided to do, Tom would need Fog healthy and well-rested. He watched the dumb brute as Angel led it away. The way the white hairs swirled along his gray coat, like . . . fog. He was very fond of the big dolt. With nowhere else to go, Tom crossed the street and went to the big yellow building, the Foothill saloon. He saw no sign of Jeff, nor of the owner, Mr Jefferson. He did, however, see Lee Tremaine at a corner table listlessly playing a game of solitaire. The only other men in the place were the old prospector Tom had seen earlier at Carrie's Kitchen, a ranch hand Tom did not recognize, and a pot-bellied red-faced man in the last stages of dissolution. No one was speaking. Tom wandered toward the bar.

'Seen Jeff around?' he asked the bartender who

was slight, had his dark hair slicked back with oil and wore German silver armbands.

'Who?'

'The new-hire swamper.'

'No, I wouldn't run into him on my shift. What'll you have?'

'How's the beer here?'

'Green and kind of sawdusty-tasting. But we keep it cool,' the bartender said with a faint smile.

'Believe I'll have a beer.' Tom waited for the man to return with a mug of pale beer and then asked casually. 'I hear there was a disturbance here last night.'

'It's an odd night that we don't have a disturbance,' the barkeep said, planting his elbows on his side of the counter.

'This was a killing disturbance,' Tom said, keeping his voice low. He saw the bartender's eyes flicker toward the table where Lee Tremaine sat.

'You a relative or a friend of the departed?'

'No. Just curious.'

'Save your curiosity for something worth being curious about,' the bar man recommended, turning away.

It was probably good advice. Tom had no need to know anything about last night's occurrences, and it was obvious that Lee Tremaine instilled either friendship or fear or both in the people of Flapjack. No one wanted to see the gambler in any trouble if they could avoid it.

Tom had a bare half-inch of beer left in his mug when the doors to the Foothill swung open and three men traipsed in. One of them he recognized as the bald owner of the saloon, Horace Jefferson. The other two looked prosperous and self-important. All three dressed well. To Tom's surprise the three walked directly toward him.

'Tom Dyce?' Jefferson said, stretching out a chubby hand. Tom nodded, accepted what seemed to be a bunch of cool sausages in his grip and waited expectantly. 'Can we sit at one of the tables? We have some business we'd like to discuss with you.'

SIX

The three, who turned out to be, besides Jefferson, a man named Walt Paulsen who owned a feed-and-grain store and William Asher, who owned the dry-goods store and several plots of land around the center of town. What they wanted to talk about became obvious as soon as the four sat down at a corner table.

'We hear you used to live around here,' Asher said slowly. He was a man with a turkey neck whose hands trembled as he spoke.

'I used to be ramrod on the Rafter T up along the high valley of the Thibido.'

'Then, we understand, you went into law enforcement,' Walt Paulsen, an over-assured man said, leaning forward across the table.

'Deputy marshal in Rincon for about a year,' Tom answered uneasily. He already had a bad feeling about this conversation.

'You see,' Jefferson said, running his hand across the hairless scalp. 'For some time now we have been considering establishing local law-enforcement in Flapjack. Frankly, we have attracted a rather rough breed of men lately.' Tom thought the saloon owner's eyes flickered briefly in the direction of the gambler, Lee Tremaine, whose own eyes remained fixed on his arranged cards.

'We can't have the town descend into lawlessness,' the jerky voice of William Asher said a little too loudly, 'just when it's showing signs of revitalization.'

'We each have wives and children,' Asher said in a tone that suggested he was responsible for all of it. 'We hope to have a school built here by next year, and we are looking into starting a fire brigade. However, the town cannot grow without first establishing law and order.'

Tom nodded and finished his beer. 'Who suggested me for the job?'

'Tarquinian Stottlemeyer, who says he knows you well.'

Tom smiled. He had thought he would never

hear that name again. 'He doesn't know me that well,' Tom said with a shrug.

'Well, Marshal Joe Adderly down in Rincon seems to,' Walt Paulsen said. In response to Tom's raised eyebrow, the feed-and-grain man said, 'Flapjack is not entirely cut off from the world, Dyce. We wired Rincon and Marshal Adderly sent back a message,' Paulsen withdrew a folded telegram from his coat pocket, 'in which he states that he has "complete faith in you, that you have his highest regard as a law officer".'

Nice of Joe, but Tom did not wish to become a law officer ever again. He rose suddenly, saying, 'I don't think I can consider your offer at this time, gentlemen. Unfortunately, I have other obligations.' Then he turned on his heel and walked away from the trio. Lee Tremaine, who must have heard at least a part of the conversation, followed him with those cold eyes of his.

Outside Tom paused for a deep breath, asked a passer-by for the time and started on. It was after four o'clock. His shoulder was aching like sin, and Laura should be home in her little cabin by now.

Not knowing exactly where he was heading, Tom wandered into the narrow alley behind the restaurant until he came upon four identical white cabins facing each other across a clearing in the oak grove there. A dog barked at him and continued to bark until someone shushed it. A weary-looking bay horse stood beside one of the cabins, tugging listlessly at the yellow grass, swishing its tail at the flies that taunted it.

Tom found the cabin with the letter 'C' crudely painted on its door and tapped at it. In moments, the door swung open and Laura stood there, smiling out at him.

'I wasn't sure you'd come,' she told Tom, escorting him inside the musty cabin. She left the door open for air.

'I wasn't either,' Tom said, taking a seat on a rust-colored plush sofa that looked older than Flapjack, and possibly was. 'I thought I'd better, though.' He rubbed his shoulder gingerly.

'Still bothering you?' Laura asked.

'It's gotten worse, actually. Now it's stiffening as well as hurting.'

'We'd better get to it,' Laura said, nodding her head toward a cubbyhole of a kitchen. 'Out there. Take off your shirt – if you can.'

Tom unbuttoned his shirt and then found that when he tried to stretch his arm out it would not co-operate. 'I guess I could use some help,' Tom told Laura, who nodded and came to help him, her lips pursed inquisitively as she studied the wound.

'Sit at the table,' Laura, all efficiency now, told him. 'I'll probably have to soak the bandages free first with some hot water before I can cut them off. They're scabbed over.'

'I'm in your hands,' Tom said as he watched her pull out a pot, fill it from the indoor pump at the sink and somehow prod the fire in the stove to life. She was all concentration. She was near enough in the small kitchen that he caught hints of her scent as she worked. Lilac, he thought, but was not sure. And he could see the small tendrils of reddish hair that curled on the nape of her neck because of perspiration. He noticed her capable hands, narrow waist. She was, he thought, a fine-looking young woman. Laura seemed unaware of his appraising glances, but she might not have been. Women, Tom thought, always knew when a man was looking at them with interest. Laura was carefully unwrapping the bandages that she could – those not pasted down by clotted blood. She made small sounds of distaste as she worked. Tom was aware of her small exhalations brushing over his flesh.

'Well, whoever did this did well enough, but obviously he had little experience,' Laura said assessing Wade Block's patch job.

'He's only a ranch hand. That's probably the way he stitches a steer that has torn itself on barbed wire.' Tom smiled at his own remark, but the smile was overwhelmed by pain as Laura went too far with her tugging at the dirty bandage.

'Sorry – that must have hurt. I've started it bleeding, and I see some pus. I'm afraid I'm going to have to pull out these old stitches, clean the wound and start all over again.'

'If you have to,' Tom muttered. He had been hoping for a quick fix.

'I have to if you want the wound clean and ready to heal properly,' Laura told him, adopting a motherly tone.

'Go ahead,' Tom said unhappily. He knew what removing Wade Block's stitches, opening the wound and applying new stitchery was going to feel like. But if Laura thought it had to be done, may as well let her get started. As she worked and the pot whistled on the stove, they talked between Laura's concerned puffs of breath and Tom's occasional grunt of pain.

'Are you still planning on taking the stagecoach

on Saturday?' Tom asked.

'Yes! The day after tomorrow,' she said happily.

'You said there was a layover in Rincon.'

'Yes, and that's where you came from, isn't it? Do you know of a place to stay?'

'There's a hotel there,' Tom told her.

'Oh, yes! Rincon's a big town, isn't it?'

'If you're from Flapjack, I suppose it is,' Tom answered, wincing as Laura pulled out the last stitch Wade Block had put in.

'Let me kind of open it up, and then I have some salve to put on the wound,' Laura said.

'Open it up. . . ?' Tom began, but then he winced with pain and felt perspiration pop out of his forehead as, with a pair of tweezers, Laura peeled back the wound's flaps of skin. She was against his back now, talking a near-whisper.

'Saturday for me,' she said as her fingers worked. 'What about you, Tom? Are you staying or leaving?'

'Staying, for a while, I think. I still have some unfinished business.' Without meaning to, he drifted into the long story of Aurora Tyne and her ranch, about his suspicions concerning Ray Fox. Laura was cleaning the open wound with a cloth. Tom could feel blood leaking down his arm. He began talking again, to distract himself from what she was doing. After a time he could hear himself telling Laura how lovely Aurora was, how she had rejected him. He knew a man doesn't go around telling one woman how attractive he finds another, but the words just seemed to spill from his lips.

'She's the tall lady with the long dark hair, isn't she? I've seen her two or three times in the restaurant.' Her voice seemed indifferent, but Tom thought he heard some other emotion lurking in her words. He shrugged off his pointless conjectures. Painfully, Laura swabbed out his gunshot wound with lye soap and then produced a mixing bowl and what looked to be a pestle.

'What's that?' Tom asked. He thought he recognized the small white berries, but could not be sure.

'Mistletoe,' Laura answered, smashing the berries to a paste. 'Indians use it all the time for treating wounds. That and green moss which helps the wound to coagulate – we'll skip that part, you're not bleeding heavily.'

'Where did you learn about that?' Tom asked. He recalled once being told about mistletoe from an old plainsman, but it wasn't common knowledge.

'Back home I had a woman who was part Crow Indian as a nurse when I was young.' Laura was applying the paste to his wound now. 'I was interested in Indian medicine long before I thought of becoming a nurse myself. Does that hurt?'

'No, it's soothing actually,' Tom said.

'Good,' she said reaching for a needle and waxed thread, 'because what I am going to do next *will* hurt, I can guarantee.'

Now she was the one who talked as she pieced the skin on Tom's shoulder together again. 'I heard that you were going to be offered the job of town marshal.'

'It's not the job for me,' Tom said through clenched teeth as Laura took another stitch.

'No, I suppose not, but I was thinking – if you are determined to halt the feud between the Rafter T and Circle R for Aurora, and to find out the truth about Ray Fox, to nab Vance Wynn – wouldn't it be easier to accomplish all that if you were wearing a badge?'

'It would . . . ow!' Tom cried out, half-rising from his chair.

'Sit still,' Laura admonished him. 'You don't want this shoulder to look like a piece of quiltwork when it heals, do you?'

'No,' Tom said through clenched teeth. 'As I was trying to say – the long valley is far outside of Flapjack's town limits. I can't see how a marshal's badge could help anything.'

'Maybe not, but it lends a little authority to your poking around.'

'I can't see myself taking up residence in Flapjack,' Tom said, wincing again. 'You know how that would be – it's the reason you're leaving.'

'Yes, I know, but you could explain to the town council that it was only a temporary move until they find someone who really wants the job.'

'I suppose so,' Tom said doubtfully, hunching his shoulders as he waited for the next piercing of the needle. But Laura stood back, brushed her hair from her forehead and said with a triumphant cry:

'Finished! That's it except for a fresh bandage, and I believe the patient will make a full recovery.'

Tom glanced at his shoulder. It was puffy and bruised, but it looked better than the last time he had seen it. He would have to trust to Laura's herbal remedy to fight the infection.

'You should try to move it as little as possible for the next few days,' Laura said, and, surprising Tom, she ruffled his hair familiarly. 'Your cowhand days are over for a while.'

Was she hinting that he ought to consider the marshal's job? Perhaps she was right. He had to do something to support himself, and his savings would not last long.

After Laura finished her kitchen cleaning they sat on a bench circling an old oak in the back of the cabin, drinking coffee and talking of many things, most of them inconsequential. He found she was easy to talk to, with a quick wit. The image she had first presented to him was that of a totally different young woman.

When the color began to paint the sky in the west, Tom rose to his feet. Laura took his hands and looked up with misted eyes. He wondered for a moment if he was supposed to kiss her, but the invitation wasn't clear enough.

'Thanks for the medical help, Laura. You're a woman with many hidden gifts.'

'Yes, Tom, I am,' she said.

'Well, I've got matters to attend to,' Tom said uneasily, and Laura let her hands drop away.

'I know. Goodbye, Tom, you know I must leave soon.'

Tom Dyce trudged back toward town, thinking about Laura. He had the feeling that she was speaking of many things at once. He knew that she was leaving Saturday; her words seemed to be a forever farewell, and he supposed they were. He had never learned the ways of women; he supposed he never would.

Horace Jefferson himself was tending bar in the Foothill saloon when Tom Dyce tramped in. The place was still fairly silent at this time of the evening. Lee Tremaine had engaged three other men in a game of poker. The prospector still sat at one table, asleep, head on his arms.

'Quiet night,' Tom remarked to Jefferson who lifted his eyes questioningly.

'They come and go,' Jefferson said. 'What can I do for you?'

'I guess one of those green and cool beers. Then – I'd like to talk business with you. I've been reconsidering the offer you gentlemen made me.'

'You'll take the job of town marshal?' Jefferson asked with surprise.

'On a strictly temporary basis,' Tom said.

'Well. . . .' Jefferson was stuck for words. 'Wait until my regular bartender comes in, and we'll go see Asher and Paulsen. I think they'll approve.'

Later they emerged from the saloon, Jefferson hurriedly putting on his coat as they walked. 'This is wonderful,' he panted. 'It's getting wild around here, too wild.'

'I haven't noticed much trouble.'

'You only just arrived.'

'True.'

'That shooting incident in my place the other night was hardly an isolated incident, Dyce. There's nights – days – that bullets are flying around the street regardless of whether women and children are about. We just can't have that sort of behavior in Flapjack anymore,' Jefferson said definitely.

The meeting was held at the house of the prosperous feed-and-grain store owner, Walt Paulsen. It was a fancy structure for this far west: two-storied, of white clapboard with green-painted shutters and doors. The interior approached luxurious. Plush chairs, walnut tables and polished floors. Paulsen had done very well for himself indeed.

Tom Dyce heard a woman's voice, but she did not show herself as they traipsed into Paulsen's study where he sat behind a broad desk covered with business invoices. His eyes were fixed upon Tom as were those of William Asher. Horace Jefferson sat silently in a corner chair, hat on his lap.

'I understand that you have reconsidered our offer, Dyce; that you will agree to be our town marshal.'

'On a temporary basis,' Jefferson spoke up.

'Oh?' Paulsen's heavy eyebrows drew together. 'We really are looking for a permanent marshal.'

'Have you someone in mind?' Tom asked with a faint smile. 'Keep on looking, and I'll hold down the job until you find someone.'

'It's a start.' William Asher said in his squeaky voice.

'I see,' Paulsen, who seemed to have taken the council lead, said. 'What sort of wages are you expecting, Dyce?'

'Whatever you are preparing to offer to a permanent marshal less ten per cent.'

'I'll agree to that,' Jefferson said, his bald head glistening with lamplight. 'Make it forty a month, then. Is that all right, Dyce?'

'It will do.'

'When can you start?' Asher asked. 'There's already been trouble on the streets tonight.'

'As soon as I get a new shirt to pin the badge on,' Tom said, displaying the ripped blue shirt he now wore. His bandages could be seen through the split shoulder seam. 'And after we've settled a few things.'

'You're setting conditions?' Walt Paulsen asked, his frown deepening.

'Trying to settle matters,' Tom said easily. 'Things your new marshal will have to take care of if I don't do it now – a jail, for instance. And a room for me to stay in.'

'A jail?' Asher said it as if it were a shock. His turkey neck quivered doubtfully.

'You've got to have a place to lock up the drunks and brawlers. What am I supposed to do? Tie them to a tree somewhere?'

'I suppose. . . .' Paulsen drummed his chubby fingers on his desk top. 'I've got an empty room in my warehouse and another that could be cleaned out without a lot of work. The walls are heavily timbered.'

'What about the doors?' Jefferson asked with a hint of uneasiness. 'I wouldn't want to have one of the roughnecks arrested only to have him break out and come back mad an hour later.'

Tom suggested. 'Why can't you get the blacksmith, Bridgeport to reinforce the doors with iron straps, whatever stock he has handy? The man seems to know what he's doing. Down the line he could fashion steel bars for a real jail door. He'd be glad to get the work, I think.'

'I have that small parcel of land behind the stable,' William Asher said, growing more eager. 'Land sales have been more than a little slow. Why not build a new jail on the property? It seems we are going to need one sooner or later.'

'That takes time,' Paulsen muttered. 'For now, we'll go the way Dyce suggests. I'll talk to Bridgeport in the morning, see what he thinks he can do.' His eyes leveled once again on Tom's. 'Anything else, Dyce?'

'Yes, there is,' Tom told him, looking at each of the three members of the town council in turn. 'What are we calling the town limits of Flapjack? I have to know my boundaries.'

'Well. . . .' Paulsen seemed momentarily flustered. 'It's never come up before. You obviously have a reason for asking us to define the town limits.'

Tom said quietly, 'There's trouble brewing up along the Thibido.'

'Yes, we've all heard. But those ranches up on the long valley . . . why, they're miles away! We can't include them in the town limits.'

'Why would we want to?' Asher asked almost delicately.

'You want us to hire a marshal to guard the ranch properties? No,' Paulsen said firmly. 'Why would we care about their squabbles?'

'Because they could very quickly become your own,' Tom said, leaning forward. 'If they get to feuding up there, you may see a lot of new arrivals in Flapjack, and not the sort of men you are hoping to see. Thugs, hired guns looking for rough work. They'll be hanging around Flapjack, drinking in the Foothill saloon. If you think these local boys are tough, wait until someone gets it in his mind to hire a bunch of Texas toughs.'

'It could happen,' Horace Jefferson said miserably. 'Those boys don't care about anything but whiskey, women and money. And women would be coming too – not the sort we want. They could tear this town down while we watched all of our decent citizens depart.'

'What makes you think you could stop this, Dyce?'

'I want to take care of matters out on the range before it ever gets to that point, before things boil over and spill into Flapjack.'

'I see. What do you think we could do, Bill?' Paulsen asked Asher. The narrow man was shaking his head. His eyes brightened slightly.

'We *could* simply annex the ranches.'

'Annex? Art Royal would have a fit!'

'It would build up our tax base,' Jefferson said. 'Circle R and Rafter T have the use of our town without ever having paid a dollar in taxes. We could take a vote on that – I'd say "yes".'

'I don't know if it's even legal,' Paulsen said stubbornly.

'Neither do I. Neither does Art Royal or Aurora Tyne. By the time they could bring the matter before any judge, months will have passed. And if Dyce has cleaned up that mess by then, we'll simply drop the annexation and apologize.'

'Why do I feel like I'm being railroaded?' Walt Paulsen asked, his accusing eyes on those of Tom Dyce. Then he said in frustration, 'All right, then – as of this moment the Thibido Creek long valley is considered to be within the boundaries of the town of Flapjack. We'll draw up the annexation papers, legal or not.

'Dyce, if you have a plan for settling that trouble up there, I'd be obliged if you got to it as quickly as possible.'

After briefly examining the rooms in Walt Paulsen's feed-and-grain warehouse, which were marginally suitable – one of them even having a cot in it – Tom accompanied William Asher back up town to his dry-goods store where he purchased a blood-red shirt, tossing his other away.

Then, without ceremony, Tom pinned on the town marshal's badge and went out to look over his new domain.

Gunshots rang out as he stepped into the street and he swung around to see the bartender of the Foothill saloon running out of the building, waving his hands skyward.

'It's Lee Tremaine! He's gunned down our swamper!'

Jeff?

Spinning on his heel, Tom walked toward the saloon where wisps of gunsmoke could be seen curling out above the batwing doors, and stepped up onto the porch, his eyes narrowed, his mouth set grimly.

SEVEN

Jeff Stottlemeyer, wearing a white apron, was sprawled against the floor of the Foothill saloon in a puddle of beer and blood. It was difficult to tell if he was alive or not. Lee Tremaine sat behind a card table, his cold eyes flickering toward Tom. There seemed to be a faint smile on the corners of Tremaine's mouth. Perhaps because he knew that no one in town would be eager to testify against him at a trial. Tom looked again at Jeff – he had no gun. Why Jeff would have had a problem with Tremaine, Tom could not guess. Had he been gambling? Not wearing his work apron, he hadn't. Tom stood in front of Tremaine now as a couple of men moved Jeff to a back room.

Lee Tremaine's dark eyes flickered up, pausing

briefly on the silver badge Tom now wore.

'What seems to be the trouble, Marshal?' Tremaine asked, managing to make the last word a mocking appellation.

'You just shot a man, Tremaine. I'm taking you in for murder, or attempted murder, depending on whether your victim survives.'

'Taking me in!' Tremaine said, spreading his hands, one of which still held a deck of cards. 'Where?'

'We've made arrangements.'

'Listen ... Marshal ... things aren't as they might seem. Why don't you sit down and we'll talk about it.' Tremaine pushed a chair toward Tom with his boot.

Sit down? Not likely. Tom knew how Lee Tremaine carried his gun – in a holster sewn to the side of his boot. 'No, I'll tell you what. Tremaine, you stand up and come along with me.'

Tremaine placed his deck of cards down, cocked his head as if thinking matters over and suddenly blurted out, 'I don't think so!' And Tremaine tried to get to his feet as he made a grab for his awkwardly positioned gun. Tom leaned away and drew his Colt. Before Tremaine's gun had cleared the table top, Tom had shot him twice. The gambler staggered back, tipped over the chair he had been sitting in and fell to the floor, his gun clattering free.

'Nice work,' someone muttered and Tom turned his head enough to see the owner of the bar, Horace Jefferson, looking his way, nodding his head in approval. A man was crouched over Tremaine's body. He looked up shaking his head.

'Here's one for the blacksmith,' the man said rising.

Tom put his gun away shakily. He had been lucky – with the shape his arm was in, he thought, any man in the room could have outdrawn him. Except for the man who wore his pistol on his boot.

Jefferson had stepped from behind the bar to approach Tom. He put his meaty hand on Tom's shoulder. 'You're already paying dividends, Dyce. I've been trying to figure out how to get rid of Lee Tremaine for months.'

'Thanks,' Tom said dully. 'Where'd they take Jeff Stottlemeyer? I want to see how he is.'

'Jeff. . . .' Jefferson's face went blank. 'Oh, Tarquinian. The boys took him into the storeroom. That way,' he nodded. 'It doesn't look good for him.'

'I'll see. Will you arrange for a couple of men to take Tremaine over to Bridgeport's blacksmith shop?'

'Sure, I'll do that, Marshal,' Jefferson said, and when he used the last word there was no hint of disparagement.

Tom strode across the room, men parting to make a corridor for him. A general conversation broke out behind him as he entered the hallway leading to the store room.

Only a single man remained beside Jeff, who lay on a plank placed on top of two beer kegs. The man glanced up, bloody towel in his hand. It was the drunk Tom had seen in the Foothill before. With watery eyes he studied Tom and then looked back to the still form of Jeff Stottlemeyer.

'Has he a chance?' Tom asked.

'I hope so. He's the only man in the place who ever treated me like a human being,' the drunk answered. 'I've been trying to clean him up, but I can't stop the bleeding.'

'Where'd he get tagged?'

'Low on the right side. If the bullet didn't hit liver or kidney, he might have a chance – if the bleeding can be stopped. What he needs is a doctor.'

'We don't have one,' Tom said. But they had the next best thing. 'Go get two strong men. We're going to move him.'

'Do you think that's a good idea?'

'I don't know if there is a good idea right now, but that's what we're doing. Go find two men.'

Laura had been folding some clothing she meant to take on the Saturday stage when there was a pounding on her door. She looked up with surprise, frowned and walked to open it. Outside the cottage door she found a group of men, Tom Dyce at their head. One of the men was injured. They had placed him on a plank and transported him to her place that way.

'Can we come in, Laura?' Tom asked. 'It's important.' Tom's face was pale, drawn.

'I can see that. Come in.' She stepped aside, motioning with her arm for the others to follow. 'You can put him on my bed. This way.'

They followed her to her room, and after she finished clearing the bed of her neatly folded clothing, they lowered Jeff onto it. Laura took a quick look at the wound, nodded and said, 'All of you who can't help, clear out! I'll need some room to work.'

'Thanks, boys,' Tom said to those who had carried Jeff.

'It's all right, Marshal. Just hope the man makes it.'

Laura's eyes lifted at hearing Tom addressed as 'Marshal', but she said nothing, not just then. 'Needle and thread, green moss, scissors, hot water and basin, mistletoe paste, plenty of bandaging,' she said to herself as she brushed past Tom and scurried to the kitchen.

'Can you help him?' Tom asked when she returned with her arms loaded with supplies.

'I don't know. I haven't tried yet,' she said a little sharply. 'Why don't you wait out in the other room? I'll call you if I need help rolling him over. Listen for the tea-kettle boiling.'

'All right,' Tom said meekly backing from the bedroom as Laura lifted Jeff's shirt and unbuckled his belt. Tom felt about as necessary as a fifth leg on a dog. It was humbling. He was recalled only twice, once to help Laura turn Jeff over, once to bring a kettle of hot water.

Over an hour later Laura emerged from the room. There was blood on her apron and on her hands. With the back of her wrist she wiped back the lank strands of red hair from her forehead, smiled faintly at Tom, and went to wash up.

'Has he a chance?' Tom asked, watching her at the sink.

'I don't know – a little action on the water pump if you don't mind – he's still alive, so there's always a chance. I've never done anything close to that before, Tom.' The water stopped flowing again and she dried her hands on a clean towel. 'Why do men inflict so much damage on one another?'

'I don't know,' Tom said, feeling suddenly guilty. Had he not just done the same thing himself? If Lee Tremaine had survived his wounds, would he have brought him to Laura as well? He doubted it.

'Can you imagine what an army surgeon sees?' Laura said with a shudder. 'We had a retired army doctor in my home town. People used to wonder why he showed more interest in thinking himself to death than setting up a practice. I think I know now.' She spun around and changed the subject abruptly.

'I see you've taken on a new profession.' Her eyes were fixed on the shining badge he wore. Her lips were pursed, her eyes glittering. Tom could not read that expression.

'I thought I'd help out for a little while.'

'I hope you don't get yourself hurt again, Tom.'

'I told you that I was trying to straighten out a few things. Thinking over what you said, having a badge didn't seem like such a bad idea.'

'What things?' Laura asked as she led him back to the front room. 'You mean the cattlemen's troubles?'

'Partly,' Tom answered with a shrug.

'You took on the job you don't want – for the sake of Aurora Tyne,' Laura said, sitting on the worn old sofa with a sigh.

'I guess partly. Yes, I did!'

'Why, Tom? You told me the woman doesn't want you, that she has a new man. Are you trying to find a way to win her back?' Her deep-blue eyes were steady and probing.

'I still feel that I owe her *something*. What, I don't know,' he said seating himself beside Laura. 'Does that make sense?'

'Do you know what day tomorrow is?' Laura asked, abandoning the subject. 'It's Saturday.'

'It is, isn't it?' What she was telling him slowly sunk in. 'Oh, you have a ticket on the stage.'

'Yes, and I'm using it,' she said with a hint of defiance.

'Well, it's what you'd made your mind up to do – what you wanted.'

Laura shook her head pityingly. 'Yes, that's it.'

'What time does the coach leave?'

'Not until noon. That'll give me time to see to the wounded man again and find someone to take care of him.'

'Jeff's got a room at the saloon.'

'I don't think he should be moved again. Not so soon.'

'No, I guess not,' Tom said, feeling the conversation wind down. He got to his feet.

'I didn't figure you'd be around in the morning to look after him,' Laura said, rising to join him.

'No, I've got to be riding up to the Thibido Creek country. The sooner I start taking care of matters up there, the better.'

'I'll find someone who'll sit with Jeff for a few dollars. Do you have a place to sleep tonight?'

'Yes. In my new office,' Tom answered.

'Oh?' she said curiously. 'I didn't know you had one. Never mind.' She took his hand and said, 'Good luck to you, Tom.' Then she rose to tiptoes and kissed him lightly, warmly, turned and walked back to the kitchen, leaving him stunned and confused. Walking out into the coolness of the evening he glanced skyward at the sliver of the new moon in a sky that was dark, still and solemn.

Shaking off his mood, he stalked back to the feed-and-grain warehouse and found his 'office'. Tom lay down on the shaky cot, hands behind his bed, hearing the faint scuttling of mice which probably infested the hay-strewn building.

There was little light in his room and he closed his eyes to try to sleep. Oddly he could still feel the touch of Laura's warm lips lingering on his. A man can be such a fool! Eventually he curled up, threw his blanket across his legs and fell to sleep.

Less than an hour after dawn Tom Dyce guided Fog into the long grassy valley along the silver-bright Thibido Creek. The tips of the pines along the ridge were limned with gold as if a rank of Christmas trees were standing there. The shadows were cool beneath the canopy of oak trees as Tom rode across the yard. He could smell frying bacon in the air and the scent of coffee. No one was about. The yard dog emerged from beneath the porch, barked twice and ambled off, having done its duty.

The front door opened and Aurora appeared. She wore a white blouse and denim trousers. She watched Tom's approach, arms folded. Eventually she waved.

'Hello, Tom, we thought you'd abandoned us!'

'I had some business to take care of,' he said, swinging down and loosely hitching Fog to the rail. Aurora's eyes narrowed. She was looking at his badge.

'I see. You don't waste much time, do you?'

'It's only temporary. They wanted to find someone to pin a badge on.'

'I see,' Aurora said with a tone that meant she didn't see. 'Come on in. I've fresh coffee. Ray is just finishing his breakfast. If you'd like anything. . . .'

'No, thanks. I'm all right,' Tom said although his stomach was calling him a liar.

In the kitchen Ray Fox was just finishing his meal. He wiped his mouth with a white napkin and leaned back in his chair. He, too, saw the badge pinned to Tom's red shirt.

'You do get around, don't you?' he said, a smile creasing his handsome face.

'A man's got to keep moving,' Tom said. If Fox caught the meaning in his words, he showed no sign of it.

'Well, I still haven't found those missing calves. I'm giving it another try this morning. Want to ride with me, Tom?'

'Sure, be glad to.'

'Ask Art Royal where they are,' Aurora said with a little bitterness.

Ray Fox went to her and took her in his arms from behind. He bent his face and kissed her on the neck. Tom felt baseless jealousy rise. Ray Fox seemed to sense eyes on him, for he released Aurora and told Tom:

'I sent Juan out to saddle my horse. Let me grab my rifle and I'm ready.'

'All right, I'll be out front,' Tom answered.

'Sure you don't want a quick cup of coffee?' Laura asked.

'No. I'd better get going,' Tom replied.

She shrugged as if it were of no importance to her and got back to her sink. Tom had hoped to have a word or two with Aurora, but about what? He heard the sound of the returning Ray Fox's boots clicking against the floor and he turned to leave the house. The time for talking had gone, it seemed.

Ray Fox was mounted on a leggy sorrel horse when the two men left the ranch yard. Aurora stood on the porch, watching them go with unreadable eyes. Tom thought that it was the badge he wore that concerned her. If it bothered her, it didn't seem to faze Ray Fox at all. He never mentioned it again – of course, that didn't mean he wasn't thinking about its significance.

'You know this country, Tom. Can you think of a place we might not have looked?'

'Do you know the Sugar Bowl?' Tom asked as Ray slowed his eager horse to ride beside the plodding Fog.

'No. I've only been here a month or so. That's why I asked you along,' Fox said, tilting back his hat so that a fringe of dark curly hair escaped onto his forehead.

'Sugar Bowl is a tiny valley, a sink really, what some call a teacup valley, a few miles east. I thought of it because it's out of any normally traveled route, and because of its form. The sides aren't really all that steep, but they might be enough to convince a spindly young calf that it wasn't worth trying to scale – especially if they were already tired from being driven hard. That, and there's usually a pencil-thin rill running along the bottom.'

'All right,' Ray Fox agreed. 'Let's have a look.'

An hour on they came to something that caught their attention. Ray Fox, frowning, pulled up on his sorrel and sat letting his eyes search the ground. 'Am I seeing what I think I am?' Fox asked Tom.

'It looks that way.' For now they could clearly see the sign of four or five young cattle being driven from the south, and from the north, where there was another cut in the wire fence, three or four others. 'They're being driven from both sides of the wire. Your calves and Art Royal's.'

'And we've been accusing each other,' Ray said unhappily. 'Tom, it looks like we've both got a couple of traitors riding for us, wouldn't you think?'

'It seems that way. There are too many new-hires working up here. It seems a few of them got together and figured out a way to make their own start.'

'Maybe they knew each other before and had this planned out.'

'It could be – but it looks like Art and Aurora owe each other an apology. Let's string a rough fix on those barbed wire strands and then ride on. It seems that we must be headed in the right direction,' Tom said, tugging on his gloves.

In fifteen minutes they were back in the saddle, heading toward the Sugar Bowl again. Remote, it lay beyond the boundaries of either ranch. It was the place Tom would have chosen himself if he were a rustler. They entered thick pine forest and were briefly hidden in the cool shadows.

Even before they had emerged from the woods they could hear the sounds of a bewildered calf bawling. A man shouted sharply and another answered. Ray Fox pointed at a narrow, wind-flagged column of smoke.

'Branding time,' he mouthed at Tom, and removed his Winchester from its saddle scabbard. They walked their horses across the grassy clearing between them and the rim of the Sugar Bowl, each carrying a rifle across his saddlebow now. To their left they saw two riderless horses, left to graze on the flats.

They rode to the very lip of the Sugar Bowl, and looking down they could see fifty or so calves, four men and a low-burning fire with running irons heating in it. One calf had already been thrown and tied and this was the one bawling wildly.

'Ain't those irons hot yet?' one of the men called with a sense of urgency.

Tom started his horse toward the concave slope of the valley. A narrow path was visible, evidently the one used by the rustlers. Ray Fox asked in an anxious whisper:

'What are you going to do, Tom?'

'Arrest them, I guess,' Tom answered, and he

kneed Fog forward. Ray Fox muttered an unintelligible word and gripped his rifle more tightly, following Tom Dyce into the teacup valley.

EIGHT

One of the men held a running iron in his gloved hands as he approached the writhing calf that was being held down by an accomplice. He wore leather chaps and a black-and-white checked shirt. The man holding the calf down lifted his head at the sound of approaching horses and Tom saw his eyes open wide.

Sounding clearly, sharply above the clopping of the horses' hoofs came the sound of Ray's Winchester rifle's lever ratcheting a shell into the receiver. The men stood watching sullenly. Ray Fox's sorrel horse was acting jittery and it suddenly side-stepped until it was far too close to the man in the chaps. His hand shot out and grabbed the horse's bridle.

The sorrel danced away, and Fox, riding with his rifle in his hands was thrown from its back to land roughly on the ground. Before he could rise, the man in the chaps and black-and-white shirt was on top of him. They rolled down the slope and into the mud, bordering the little silver rill as the calves scattered and the tied dogie continued to bawl. Tom, sitting the stolid Fog, kept his rifle trained on the other three men. There was no chance of taking a decent shot at the man who had attacked Ray, tangled up as the two were.

'Just stand easy, men,' Tom warned the others. They eyed him darkly as Ray Fox suddenly got the upper hand, rising to his feet to drive two stunning blows into the rustler's face. The man staggered back, hands windmilling, and fell on his back into the rill. Ray, his shirt torn, his face and hands covered with mud, started back to join Tom. Before he reached the knot of men the three remaining rustlers had begun to spread out, their hands close to their holstered pistols.

The man on the ground slowly rose, shaking the water from his hair. On hands and knees he made it to the bank of the creek where he slowly rose, his eyes fierce.

One of the other three said, 'Hold it where you

are, Fox,' and drew his gun. 'You!' he shouted at Tom Dyce, 'you don't seem to be good at counting. There's four of us standing against you. If you start shooting, you haven't got a chance.'

Tom froze for a moment. They were right. He wasn't going to take down four men no matter how accurate or lucky he was. He glanced at Ray Fox, who had halted, his chest heaving with exertion, weaponless. The man he had beaten would more than likely kill Ray first while the other three aimed their weapons at Tom.

'You can count again!' someone called from the rim of the valley. Looking that way Tom saw the owner of the Circle R, Art Royal, and Wade Block sitting their horses, rifles aimed at the rustlers. 'Drop those pistols, boys, or you won't live to see tomorrow.'

Desperate looks passed between the rustlers. Then, grumbling, they unfastened their gunbelts and tossed them in to a pile. Art Royal rode down the slope, Wade Block following.

'Why, howdy, Tom!' Art called out. 'What are you doing out this way?'

'I guess I'm arresting some men,' Tom answered. Art Royal caught the shimmer of sunlight on Tom's badge, frowned and shook his head.

'That's a town marshal's badge,' one of the men said belligerently. 'You got no authority to arrest us out here!'

'I think I do,' Tom replied coolly. Art spoke up:

'We don't need your authority, Tom – whatever it may be. Jack, Wesley, you haven't been working for me long, but you have been around long enough to know that I'm an old-fashioned man, and I do things in the old-fashioned way.'

'What do you mean?' one of them, the one named Jack, asked shakily, his nerve fading.

'If I take a stray dog in and it bites my hand, I take it out and shoot it. When I take on a couple of saddle tramps because I'm short-handed and they turn out to be nothing but a pair of greedy rustlers, I string 'em up,' Art Royal said, his eyes shifting around as if looking for a tree. What do you say, Ray?' he asked Fox.

'Can't do it. Not with a lawman sitting here,' Ray answered calmly. 'I understand the feeling, though. These two men I have to claim as Rafter T riders are new-hires also. They have no loyalty to the brand but only to their pocketbooks.'

'We were only trying to get enough to start our own place, to be as lucky as you both have been,' the man named Wesley whined.

'Find your luck someplace else,' Art Royal said severely. 'If you ever show up in these parts again, I won't even look for a rope and a tree. I'll shoot you down like the ungrateful dogs you are. For now, scatter!' Art fired his rifle over their heads and, leaving their guns behind, the four rustlers raced for their horses, grateful to be escaping with their lives.

Wade Block was scooping up the weapons, placing them in his saddlebags. Art still sat his horse, but he now spoke to Ray Fox. 'I should have known that Rafter T wouldn't have been involved in something like this,' Art said. 'But it got to the point where no one was talking.'

'I'll tell Aurora that you will be coming by for supper,' Ray said, extending his hand. 'If you think you'd like to come over, Mr Royal.'

'I'd like that just fine,' Art Royal answered. Touching his hat brim with a finger, he said to Block. 'I'll send Cory Stamps and a couple of the men out to help you hie our calves home. Think you'll have them sorted out by then?'

'I'll give it a try,' Block said. 'Though damned if their faces don't all look the same to me.'

Ray laughed and asked Art Royal, 'Why don't we just split them fifty-fifty?'

126

'Sounds fair,' Art agreed. He had swung down to cut the piggin strings binding the unlucky calf. 'Makes it easier on everybody.' He picked up the running irons and threw them into the creek.

'Looks like we'd better start branding our calves a little earlier,' Ray commented. 'We can't have anyone else doing it for us. I'll send up a couple of my men to collect Rafter T's share when I get back to home ranch.'

'Even before you do that,' Tom said, 'will you explain to Aurora about what has happened? I can't stand having that woman mad at me.'

'I'll tell her first thing,' Ray promised. Then, leaving Wade Block behind with the calves, Art Royal smiled and rode up the path leading out of Sugar Bowl, a happier man than he had been on his arrival.

They watched him go. Then Ray, looking at his torn shirt, mud-stained jeans and filthy hands said, 'I guess I should rinse off a little before we start back. It'd frighten Aurora to see me dragging in looking like this.'

Ray found a spot where the rill barely trickled past. A nearly flat boulder sat on the bank of the creek there. Undressing, he waded into the water and began washing himself vigorously. Tom Dyce seated himself on the sun-warmed granite boulder and watched. He removed a much-folded piece of paper from his pocket and spread it flat on the rock, next to Ray Fox's clothes.

When Ray, naked, waded out of the rill, shaking his head to dry his hair, he returned with a smile to where Tom waited. He started to pick up his trousers, but his reaching hand halted halfway to them. The poster had caught his eye. Involuntarily his hand went to the small of his back where the spider-shaped scar Tom had seen was cut into his flesh. His dark eyes lifted to Tom.

'I guess you know, then?' Ray Fox said.

'I guess I do,' Tom answered.

'Mind if I get dressed?'

'Everything but your gunbelt.'

Ray nodded, tugged on his trousers and crouched to pick up his boots. 'Dyce,' he said, 'you might think you know what this is all about, but you don't.'

'Don't I?'

'Not if you're taking Sheriff Harley Griffin's word for it. You said you met him. I've got to assume that's where your information came from.'

'Are you denying that you're Vance Wynn?' Tom asked, slipping from the rock to have a better position to fight from if that became necessary.

'I don't see how I can.'

'You've been identified as the man who robbed the bank down at Ruidoso, and the man who murdered Harley Griffin's wife.'

'I figured as much. But who identified me, Dyce? Harley Griffin, that's who.'

'I wouldn't know – I wasn't there when they named you as the man who did it.'

The man called Ray Fox tightened his belt and leaned against the rock, putting his hat on.

'That poster says the reward is two thousand five hundred dollars.'

'It is. Dead or alive,' Tom said.

'I suppose that's enough to have made it worth your while,' Ray Fox said.

'I didn't come here looking for a reward,' Tom said. They both heard small sounds and glanced to where Wade Block was aimlessly throwing pebbles into the creek, still waiting for riders from the Circle R to arrive and help him with the calves.

'Then why?' Fox asked.

'I heard that someone was cheating Aurora. I was told it was you.'

'You can't still think that?'

'No. But I am still wondering if it will help

Aurora more to leave you here or take you away from the ranch.'

'I think you're considering something else,' Fox said with a crooked smile. 'Whether with me gone Aurora would be more likely to take you back.'

'What do you think?' Tom asked.

'You'd have to ask her,' Ray shrugged. 'Maybe that would depend on what you told her.'

'You killed one woman,' Tom pointed out, and astonishingly Ray Fox laughed.

'I did, did I?' Ray crawled up on the flat rock and told Tom. 'Sit down and I'll tell you a story.'

Tom seated himself beside Ray, but not near enough so that the man could make a grab for his gun. Ray said:

'I never shot a woman. I never robbed a bank. Can I prove it? No. But that was the reason Harley Griffin was willing to ride so far out of his county. He wasn't trying to avenge his wife's murder. He only meant to kill me so that I couldn't tell my side of things. He never meant to have me stand trial. He wants me dead. When he decided to turn back, he chose you for the job of hunting me down.'

'But why. . . ?'

'It was the sheriff who held up the bank then rode home to hide the money and change his outfit. And to look for me.'

'For you?'

'His wife, her name was Maria, and I were good friends, you see. Harley Griffin didn't like it that Maria sometimes invited me in for coffee and a piece of pie or something. He robbed the bank because he was fed up with his job, fed up with her. Somewhere along the way he started thinking that he could get a measure of revenge by claiming that witnesses identified me as the robber. There were no witnesses. I know that because I didn't do it, Tom.'

Tom Dyce nodded thoughtfully. He was weighing Ray's words, but could not decide if he believed the man or not.

'On that day we heard Harley riding in on his lathered horse. He came into the house carrying his saddle-bags. He looked frightened, nervous. I watched him through the crack in the bedroom door.'

'He didn't know you were there?'

'No. I'd left my horse out in a cottonwood grove, like I always did when I visited Maria. I didn't want folks talking about her. Harley said a few rough words to Maria and tempers exploded. I couldn't hear it all, but he was roaring angry. Then I heard two gunshots.'

'Didn't you go out and face him?'

'I wasn't armed, and I wasn't going to challenge a man in a killing rage. I went out the window just as Harley entered the bedroom – to change his clothes or hide the money, I suppose. I made it back to my horse and lit out of there, but by then Harley had emerged from the house again. He spotted me and guessed where I had come from. That was when he decided that he would have to kill me.'

Tom remained silent, thinking. It all tied together, but was it the truth or just a well-concocted story? 'How about if we go back to Ruidoso and let you tell your story?'

'Lock me up in the Ruidoso jail?' Ray laughed again. 'I'd never live long enough to talk to judge and jury.'

'I suppose not,' Tom said glumly. 'Maybe they'd be happy if you just returned the stolen money.'

Ray frowned. 'That wasn't very kind of you, trying to trick me into admitting something I never did. If I did have any money, I'd hand it over gladly. Tom, I've got everything a man could wish for right here.'

'Aurora'

'That's right, Aurora. Look, I know that she's the real reason you rode all the way up here, not because you wanted to find Vance Wynn. Well, I'm sorry things worked out the way they did, Tom. If Aurora were twins I'd wish you could have her sister. But she isn't. She's mine and I'll do whatever it takes to keep her trust.'

'So you've never told her about Maria, either?' Tom said, hardly believing the coffee and pie part of Ray's story. He thought he knew why Ray had not been wearing a gunbelt that morning, as well. The rest of it, oddly, he did believe.

'A woman doesn't want to hear about another,' Ray said woodenly. 'Look here, Tom, what are you going to do?' As he asked they heard riders approaching from the north, from Circle R range. They saw Block rise and go over to meet the men.

'You'd better help them sort out the calves,' Tom said, slipping from the rock to stand facing Ray.

'Yes. Tom, if you wanted you could ride back to the Rafter T and have Aurora send a few of the boys up to help me drive these calves on to home range.' Tom shook his head heavily, not looking at Ray's eyes, but only at the ground. At last he answered:

133

'No, Ray. You'll have to figure that out for your yourself. I'm riding the long way back to Flapjack. I won't be crossing Rafter T land, and I won't be talking to Aurora Tyne.'

With that Tom walked back to where the ever patient Fog stood waiting, swung aboard and crossed the rill, heading for the long trail around Split Mountain, once again detouring far around Rafter T property.

When Tom reached Flapjack, he was still fretting, wondering if he had let a known killer go free just to avoid hurting Aurora. As he reached the town limits, however, his thoughts began to take on a new focus. He shouted at the first man he passed:

'What time is it?'

The man looked at his pocket watch and called back, 'Just after one!'

Tom's spirits sagged a little more. She was gone then; Laura had taken the noon stagecoach out of Flapjack. He knew that the coach had a layover in Rincon, and began to wonder about the possibility of catching up with her there. It was probably a futile pursuit, chasing a vague illusion, but much of life is just that. He had done more foolish things in his time.

First things first. He found Jeff Stottlemeyer in bed in Laura's former cabin. A man Tom did not know was posted to watch over him. Jeff himself was propped up in bed, looking almost human. He smiled weakly as Tom strode into the room.

'Are you going to make it?' Tom asked with an answering smile.

'They tell me so,' Jeff replied, his voice still weak.

Tom sat on a corner of the bed. He asked:

'Why did Lee Tremaine shoot you, Jeff? It made no sense to me.'

'Because I've got a big mouth, Tom.' Tom waited. It was clear that Jeff was still having trouble breathing. 'I was passing through to get a mop and broom to clean up a mess a couple of cowboys had made. I happened to glance over to the table where Tremaine was playing poker with four other men. It was Tremaine's deal and I saw him pull the double-shift. When the game broke off, I was returning from my mop-up job, and noticed one of the card players standing at the bar. I gave him the word.

'You boys had better watch Tremaine, he's bottom-dealing you.'

'Go on,' Tom said, after giving Jeff a drink of

water from the bedside pitcher. Jeff nodded his thanks.

'I saw this fellow go straight to Tremaine and whisper something in his ear, and Tremaine locked eyes with me. Tom, Horace Jefferson told me earlier today that the other man was not a victim, but a confederate of Lee Tremaine's. They worked their game together.'

'Bad luck,' Tom sympathized.

'As I said, I've got a big mouth. I should have just shut up and let those two go on cheating the suckers. What did I care anyway?'

'Well,' Tom said, getting to his feet, 'it doesn't matter now.'

'No,' Jeff agreed. He brightened, 'Mr Jefferson said I'd have my room back any time I felt strong enough to be moved back over there, and he said he would hold my job for as long as it took to get back on my feet. He's a pretty good man, Tom.'

'Yes, I guess he is,' Tom agreed, remembering that he had some business of his own to take care of with Horace Jefferson.

NINE

Horace Jefferson was wearing bifocals as he sat behind his desk in the office of the Foothill saloon. He looked up from the invoice he was studying to glance at Tom with surprise.

'You're back, Marshal – good to see you.' Then he noticed that Tom was not wearing his badge, that his expression was hard-set, and he frowned. 'Dyce, what's going on?'

'I came by to resign,' Tom said, placing the badge on Jefferson's desk. The saloon-keeper blinked half a dozen times in astonishment, removed his spectacles and rubbed his eyes.

'But why?'

'I told you it was only a temporary position for

me,' Tom replied.

'Yes, we knew that but for God's sake!'

'I did you people a couple of services. I got Lee Tremaine out of the way, and I've just come back from the Thibido. The ranchers have solved their problems. No one is going to be hiring any gunmen to descend on Flapjack.'

'You accomplished this all so quickly?'

'I got lucky,' Tom went on. 'I also got you people thinking about a jail so that when you do find a marshal, he'll have a reasonable chance of keeping order here.'

'Dyce, I don't know what to say. You won't reconsider?'

'No. Thank Mr Paulsen and Mr Asher for having faith in me. I've got to be going.'

'You're leaving Flapjack?'

'Yes, I am.'

'I'm truly sorry, Dyce. Do you feel that we owe you any pay?'

'For what – one day's work? If you think you owe me a few dollars, use it to take care of . . . Tarquinian.'

'All right, Dyce,' Jefferson said with resignation. He was fingering the badge. 'I suppose we'll find someone who wants the job.'

'You will,' Tom assured him. 'Sorry, but I've got to be leaving now if I'm going to make it to Rincon by dark.'

'You're going back to Rincon?' Jefferson asked, rising to shake hands. At Tom's nod, he said, 'Well, good luck to you, Dyce. In your short time here, you've done quite a bit to help us out. Good luck with your future.'

What future? Tom thought darkly as he walked back to where Fog stood, He tightened the horse's cinches. Right now his entire plan for the future began and ended with finding Laura and . . . and what? He shook his head, amazed at his own stupidity. He did not even know the girl, not really, and she was determined to return to her nursing studies.

'Got a few more miles left in you?' Tom asked Fog, rubbing the gray horse's muzzle. 'I promise you a long rest once we get where we're going.'

He swung into leather and started the plodding animal southward toward Rincon, where he hoped that somehow at least a small fragment of his future waited for him. The afternoon passed in a sun blurred haze during which Tom tried to think of absolutely nothing. He wasn't successful at that.

He continued to think of Laura and what he could say to the red-headed girl.

That he had lost Aurora and he had decided upon her? That he no longer had a job of any sort, but nevertheless she should give up her quest for her long-wanted career in nursing? That would certainly sound like a great opportunity for a young woman . . . Fog plodded on.

Reaching Rincon, he stabled Fog up. The animal was due for a long rest and decent food. He slapped the placid gray horse on the rump and stepped out into the late sunlight of Rincon. He wanted to rush to the hotel and find Laura, but his reservations about doing so held him back like an anchor. All was folly.

He crossed the street and found himself in front of the marshal's office. Tom entered, not because he felt the urge to visit Joe Adderly but more because he was delaying his visit with Laura. Joe sat behind his desk, boots on its top, hands behind his head.

'Well, I'll be damned!' Joe said, rising. He ran a hand over his thin, reddish hair and shook hands with Tom. 'I didn't expect to see you again, Tom. I thought you had a situation in Flapjack.'

'That didn't work out,' Tom Dyce told him. 'I do

thank you for sending that recommendation, though.'

'Least I could do,' Joe said with a dismissive gesture. 'But, Tom, you've picked the worst possible time to show up here again.'

'Oh?' Tom frowned. 'Why is that, Joe?'

'John Bass is back,' Adderly told him somberly, 'and kicking up just as rough as always.'

'But how. . . ?' Tom muttered in disbelief. 'The man's a murderer!'

'Yes, we know that, but the judge he faced said there was no evidence.'

'But the Chinese—'

'None of them would come forward to testify against Bass,' Joe told him. 'We thought we at least had him for assaulting a peace officer – you – but no one who was in the saloon was willing to testify to it either. As for you, well, you were gone and I wasn't in the saloon when it happened.'

'I can't believe it,' Tom said, remembering all of the effort he had expended in arresting John Bass. 'What's he been up to since he got back in Rincon?'

'A little of everything. Beating up folks he doesn't like, firing off his weapons recklessly. He's going to kill someone else if I don't lock him up

141

again, Tom. We're going after him tonight. Thankfully I have Harley Griffin to side me in the arrest.'

Tom stood there, momentarily stunned. 'Sheriff Griffin is back too?'

'Well, he's not a sheriff any more. He resigned after he got back to Ruidoso, Tom. I guess with his wife dead and all, he just didn't have the heart to go on. I'll swear him in as a special deputy for tonight, just to watch my back if John Bass goes off again.'

'He will,' Tom said.

'Yes,' Joe Adderly said softly. 'That's why . . . this time I think I'm going to have to kill the man, Tom. There's no stopping him, no reasoning with that animal. I know you don't approve of such tactics, but I think it's the only way to eliminate John Bass. As I told you long ago, there comes a killing time. John Bass is no better than a rabid wild creature. You know that as well as anybody.'

'I suppose so,' Tom said, even though the idea of shooting a man down out of hand still disquieted him. He had at least given Lee Tremaine a chance to make his move or come peaceably, probably risking his own life in the process. Maybe Joe was right with a thug like John Bass. Perhaps there was no other way.

The door to the office opened and Tom turned to see Harley Griffin in the doorway. The broad shouldered, heavy-bellied former lawman strode forward confidently and shook Joe Adderly's hand.

'Are we ready to go after that grizzly?' Griffin asked.

'Just about. You remember Tom Dyce, don't you?'

'Yes, how are you, Dyce?'

Tom felt himself bristling. 'And you remember Vance Wynn, don't you?' he asked, and the ex-sheriff frowned.

'Of course! I'll never forget the bastard who killed my wife.'

'Maria? She didn't have a chance, did she?' Tom asked, tensing.

'What is this?' Griffin asked, casting a glance at Joe Adderly, who could only shrug.

'Why is it that you suddenly quit your job, Griffin?'

'It's just . . . what makes it any business of yours!'

'I think you resigned because you don't need the job anymore, not with all the stolen bank loot.'

'Are you mad?' Griffin asked, although there was a flash of anxiety in his eyes. His red face grew redder. 'Joe, you'd better have a talk with your deputy.'

'He's not my deputy any longer,' Joe protested. 'And I don't know what he's talking about. Tom, what's gotten into you?'

'Just a little story that Vance Wynn told me,' Tom replied coldly.

'Wynn! You found him?' Griffin said. 'That's great!'

'Maybe not for you,' Tom said, stepping away from Griffin. 'You don't mind if we have a quick look in your saddlebags, do you, Griffin.'

'Whatever for? Of course I mind, Dyce!'

That finally convinced Tom that he was right. Up to now he had been gambling that the story Ray Fox had told him was true, because he wanted it to be true – for Aurora's sake. Now he was sure of his conclusions. What man with nothing to hide would object to a town marshal taking a quick peek in his saddle-bags?

'Go get 'em, Joe,' Tom said to the confused marshal. 'Everything's not on the up and up here.'

'Tom, are you crazy?' Joe Adderly asked unhappily.

'Maybe so. I'll apologize if I'm wrong. Now, get his saddle-bags, Joe.'

'I don't. . . .' Adderly looked apologetically at Griffin, but he could tell by Tom's glare that he meant business. 'All right, though I don't have a clue what this is all about.'

Adderly walked to the door and went out. Griffin had pasted on a smile. It was not a reassuring expression. 'I don't know what Vance Wynn told you. Dyce, but it has to have been a bunch of lies concocted to camouflage his own guilt.'

And it could be, Tom admitted to himself. All he had was Ray Fox's word. The ex-lawman smiled again and backed toward the marshal's desk putting his hand on the arm of the chair as if he were pulling it out to sit down. Tom's uncertainty led to inattention and before he could blink, Griffin had hurled the chair at his head and drawn his pistol. The roar of the .44 in the close confines of Adderly's office was deafening. By sheer chance the chair Griffin had thrown had hit Tom in the face and chest and then caromed off blocking the lead from Griffin's pistol.

Tom rolled aside, got to hands and knees and launched himself at Griffin from behind the desk. He hit Griffin with enough force to drive the former sheriff against the wall so that the breath was driven from him and his Colt revolver clattered free. Not willing to let up, Tom began driving his fists into Griffin's ribs and face as rapidly as he could. Griffin staggered back, his arms flailing in a useless attempt to fight back. Tom back-heeled him and the man went down hard on his back, his skull bouncing against the wooden floor with a jarring thump.

Tom stood over the downed man, his chest heaving, his own pistol now in his hand. 'You know I ought to kill you,' he panted. 'A man who murdered his own wife.'

'She was a slut,' Griffin slurred between battered lips. He did not make an attempt to rise. That was where Joe Adderly found them when he rushed back into his office, saddlebags cradled over his forearm, revolver in hand. His eyes took in the scene, searched Griffin's battered face and Tom's own bleeding head from where the chair had caught him.

'Put the gun away, Tom,' Adderly commanded, and Tom obeyed. Adderly shook his head heavily and muttered, 'You had better be right about things.'

Tom stood holding his breath as Adderly placed the saddlebags on his desk and began pulling out spare shirts, scarves and trail utensils. That was all the right-hand bag contained. The left-hand bag was a different story. The canvas bank bags were impossible to miss. Adderly pulled out four stacks of currency and laid them on his desk. After a quick count, he announced, 'Looks like fifteen – twenty thousand here. They still have the bank band around them. What have we got here, Harley?' he asked the man on the floor.

'The end of everything,' Harley Griffin blubbered, not quite crying, but close to it.

Joe Adderly, feeling betrayed, sighed and said, 'Suppose you move over to one of my cells, Harley?' His voice was still apologetic; he had trusted Harley Griffin as a friend and fellow law officer.

With a disconsolate Griffin locked securely in his cell, Joe upturned his chair and placed it behind his desk again, sitting down. 'There's a lot more to this, isn't there, Tom?'

'Nothing you need to know, and nothing that will help in his prosecution,' Tom said. 'I'd recommend that you call back the poster on Vance Wynn, though. It's obvious that he didn't rob that Ruidoso bank.'

'I'll do that,' Joe Slattery said unhappily. He rubbed his thumb and forefinger over his eyes,

'What about the dead woman?'

Tom glanced at the jail cell, 'He'll confess. He's got nothing left to protect.'

'I guess not,' Joe said. 'I hate to gut a man like that, Tom. Especially someone who was a good man, a good lawman.'

'He went over the line, Joe, far over the line.'

'Yes, well,' Joe Slattery said, rising. 'I guess I can only worry about my own town now. I have to go after John Bass, and I'm going to have to do it alone.'

Tom Dyce watched as Joe reached for his hat, took a shotgun from the rack, repositioned his gunbelt and started nervously toward the door. Then he spoke up.

'Joe, it's me that John Bass has a grudge against. I'll go with you . . . on the condition that you never ask me to pin on that deputy's badge again.'

'Thanks, Tom, I appreciate that. But you remember what I said earlier – I just might have to shoot the man down.'

With memories of the last time he had tried to exchange punches with John Bass, Tom only nodded. He knew where the deputies' badges were kept in the desk; he walked to it and took one out, pinning it to his bloody shirt.

'Let's see how it works out. Maybe Bass will come without a fuss.'

'Maybe the sun will rise in the west tomorrow,' Joe Adderly said grimly, and the two men went out into the fading light of day.

TEN

There he was. It was impossible to miss John Bass. In the third saloon they had checked, the Miners' Creek Bar, they spotted John Bass among the crowd. The Miners' Creek was a small, low-ceilinged place where the smoke hung in blue wreaths from the men's cigars and pipes. Being small it was also incredibly noisy as men joked, slapped cards down and cursed just for the hell of it. Tom Dyce, who was a little unsteady on his feet, slightly dizzy from being cracked on the head by Harley Griffin, eyed the interior of the saloon unhappily.

'It's a bad place to start cutting loose,' he said to Joe Adderly. 'Everybody's pretty closely packed together,' he went on, peering over the batwing doors. 'That shotgun could cause some mayhem.'

'They'll scatter as soon as I show them some iron,' Joe said confidently.

'You don't want to brawl with the man,' Tom said.

'No, I know that, Tom.'

John Bass could be seen drinking a mug of beer. His porcine eyes, red and protruding beneath bushy black eyebrows stared dully at the room around him. His massive arms, clothed in an undersized shirt, were folded on the table in front of him. He was breathing heavily through his flattened nose like a bull waiting to be challenged.

He would fight, given the chance. He had shown that time and again. Joe Adderly's plan was simple if brutal. 'I'll walk up to him casually and ask him to come along. If he makes a move, I'll blow his head off. Look, Tom, I know you don't like it, but you've tried taking the man the hard way; you know he won't come easy. I don't want you to do anything but watch my back.'

Studying Tom Dyce who was obviously still shaky, Adderly wondered if Tom was even up to that. There was blood on the younger man's face from the scuffle with Griffin, and an obvious purple bruise on his cheekbone where the chair had struck him.

'I have to do this myself, Tom, and I have to do it my way. It's been noticed around town that I've sent my deputies out to do the hard jobs. I can't have that sort of reputation.'

'You're calling the shots, Joe. If you say that's the way to do it, it's your play.'

'All right, I just wanted to have things clear.' Joe Adderly took a deep breath. 'Let's take the man down, Tom.'

He shoved his way through the batwing doors, Tom on his heels. They were immediately met by a smoky cloud of burning tobacco, waves of sour beer smells, the stiffer scents of cheap whiskey and of unwashed men.

Tom's eyes were fixed on Bass as they crossed the room, shouldering past the closely packed men. Tom thought he saw John Bass's red eyes flicker toward them. Then the man's lips split to show a broken-toothed yellow smile.

'He sees us,' Tom muttered to Joe Adderly. Joe only nodded. The slender, red-headed marshal seemed to be on a mission to prove something to the town, or to himself. Tom Dyce just wanted it over with before someone was forced to grapple with the bearish John Bass. Maybe Joe was right and Bass would give it up once Joe had his gun on him, but Tom had doubts. Bass seemed to think himself bulletproof. Being shot during his last arrest seemed to have had no lingering effect.

Tom kept his eyes on the huge man as Joe circled around a table toward him. Bass now recognized Tom and his bulging eyes glinted with amusement, or with anticipation. Bass would like to be given another chance at beating Tom Dyce to pulp.

Before Tom was ready for it, Joe Adderly's voice rang out across the Miners' Creek.

'Stand up, John Bass – you are under arrest!'

'Again?' Bass said through his nose without moving an inch. He laughed, or at least made that snorting noise which Tom took for laughter. Then he launched a diatribe against Joe Adderly, only half of which anyone could understand, but which contained more four-letter words than Tom had ever heard in one paragraph.

Still Bass had not moved. His heavy arms remained resting on the table as if daring Joe to try taking him. The men in the saloon seemed generally more curious than cautious. They had not scattered as Joe had predicted. Instead they hovered closely around the table, troubling Tom who had no idea which of them could be possible confederates of Bass.

Determination and concern both drifted across Joe Adderly's expression. Obviously now that the plan was meeting reality, he doubted his own willingness to go through with it – to simply shoot John Bass down.

And how many bullets would that take?

The crowd around the two men now began to joke and jibe at the marshal. Tom thought he could see the tips of the marshal's ears go red. He was sure that the pistol in Joe's hand was trembling. The men in the crowd continued to comment on the marshal having lost his nerve. Joe looked ill at ease, almost tearful. If he lost face in front of the entire saloon, Joe might as well just pack it up and leave Rincon. A lawman has to have respect, or he has nothing.

'Bass!' Tom Dyce said, striding forward. 'Get up or I'll kill you.'

'You little. . . .' Bass roared, and now he started to rise menacingly.

Tom Dyce shot him through the skull. Joe turned around to make sure that no man was going to interfere. Tom, panting heavily, stood over John Bass waiting for him to make another move, to rise from the floor, only wounded, as he had done once before, but John Bass was never going to rise again, not anywhere this side of the grave.

'I want three men to take him to the under-taker's parlor,' Tom Dyce ordered, and with some murmuring and much hesitation, three men came forward to do as he had commanded. Tom Dyce took the shaken Joe Adderly by the elbow and said loudly:

'Let's go, Marshal. We've got other work to see to!'

As they left the saloon Joe Adderly folded at the waist and threw up on the plankwalk. It was all Tom could do to keep from following suit. Inside the bar it was strangely silent. Tom put his arm around Joe's shoulder and started him along the street toward the marshal's office.

'At the last minute,' Joe said in a choked whisper, 'I couldn't do it.'

'I know,' Tom said comfortingly.

'But you—'

'Oh, hell, I was tired of the man,' Tom said.

'You broke your code to protect my reputation,' Joe Adderly said as they neared the office.

'I don't know – maybe so,' Tom answered.

Tom already had his deputy's badge in his hand as they entered the marshal's office where Harley Griffin stood at the barred door, beginning a complaint.

'Oh, shut up, Harley!' Joe said. 'I'm not in the mood to listen to you.'

With that, Joe put the shotgun he had been carrying back in the rack and sagged into his chair. Tom placed his badge on the desk and sat down on a straight-backed wooden chair, holding his bloody head in his hands.

'You want me to send for Doc Leitner?' Joe asked with concern. Tom simply shook his head.

'What about me?' Harley Griffin called from his cell. 'I was roughed up pretty good! And I haven't had a bite to eat since you threw me in here.'

'Neither has your wife,' Tom Dyce said.

'No, but Vance Wynn is eating a comfortable dinner somewhere, isn't he!'

'I hope so,' Tom answered without pity.

'Tom,' Joe Adderly said, 'I'm going to send for Sean Leitner. You're pretty banged up.'

'All right,' Tom agreed. There was a minute of silence before Joe spoke again.

'I lost my nerve,' he said miserably.

'You just didn't want to do it cold, Joe. But you were right in the first place – what else was there to do with someone like John Bass? There comes a killing time.'

'I've got a wife and two—'

'Two boys,' Tom interrupted. Another minute passed in silence.

'Tom?' the marshal inquired, 'Do you want my job? It's yours for the asking. I'm through with all of this, I think.'

'No,' Tom answered, 'I don't want your job. Thanks, Joe.'

'Well, think it over – we need someone even if it's only temporary. For myself, I'm hanging it up. I have a wife and . . .' Joe caught himself and quieted.

Tom was feeling woozy. He thought the idea of being a 'temporary' marshal was terrifically amusing. Just ask the people in Flapjack! He was smiling, but his bleeding head was still buried in his hands.

Joe Adderly, for his part, had gone out onto the plankwalk, hailed a kid and sent him for Doctor Leitner. 'I hope the town council has paid him this month,' Joe said. 'He might not even be willing to come to the jail.'

'Somebody ought to straighten that situation out,' Tom commented.

'It's a bureaucratic world,' the marshal said.

'I suppose so.' Tom was tired of conversation.

'You know, Tom,' Joe said at length, 'the Ruidoso bank put up a reward for the recovery of that stolen money. It's yours. I don't know how much it is, but it will help you get along until you can find something you want to do.'

'It's ten per cent,' Harley Griffin said from his cell, being unaccountably helpful. Griffin had become more subdued. No longer challenging, he had apparently accepted what life held for him from here on. He was a wounded prisoner and there was no shining hope in his future. The former sheriff seemed to accept that now, and was dealing only with the problems of survival. If they could not prove that he had killed his wife – and Vance Wynn was certainly not going to appear as a witness, nor would Tom Dyce try to persuade him to do so – Griffin might receive a ten-year sentence or less for the bank robbery. Any lawyer worth the name probably would be able to convince a jury that the once-honest lawman had snapped upon learning of his wife's death.

'Two thousand dollars' reward at least,' Griffin

said. 'I didn't have a chance to count all of the money myself.'

'That'd help,' Joe said to Tom. 'It's too bad you didn't get Vance Wynn as well.'

Tom did not answer.

It was another fifteen minutes before the front door opened and Doctor Leitner entered the office. He was not alone.

'Who's first?' he asked Joe Adderly who pointed to the cell. Leitner was brisk and smiling. He must have gotten paid at last. His nurse stood hesitantly in the doorway.

Tom peered up at her in disbelief. Laura! She stood watching as the doctor went to the cell, followed by Joe Adderly who carried a gun for the doctor's protection.

'You?' Tom said incredulously as the red-haired girl came to examine him.

'Of course it's me, you crazy man,' Laura said, gently fingering the gash in his face. 'I met Doctor Leitner at the hotel restaurant, and we got to talking. I told him about my medical background and he asked me if I would consider working as his assistant.'

'And you said?'

'I said "of course".'

'But what about nursing school?'

'I can probably learn more in a few months working with Doctor Leitner than I could in years at school.'

Laura smiled as she bent near to see to his latest injuries. 'Besides, you being as trouble-prone as you are – I'll always have someone to practice on, Tom Dyce.'